Charmed Life

Libby's Sweet Surprise

Charmed Life

Charmed Life
Libby's Sweet Surprise

LISA SCHROEDER

SCHOLASTIC INC.

ISBN 978-0-545-60378-2

12 11 10 9 8 7 6 5 4 3 2 1   14 15 16 17 18 19/0

Printed in the U.S.A.   40
First printing, August 2014

For Jo and Katrina, my UK experts

Chapter 1

Swirly Whirly Lollipop
a favorite through the years

$\mathcal{L}$ibby climbed the stepladder and reached for the jar of chocolate frogs. *Rebecca's favorite*, she thought. They weren't real frogs, of course — white chocolate in the shape of a frog, with green coloring. A strange candy, to be sure.

Also strange? How much her best friend, Rebecca, had changed over the course of six weeks, while Libby had been away at summer camp. Try as she might, Libby couldn't figure out what had happened while she'd been away. It was as much of a mystery to her as why someone would want to eat a piece of candy in the shape of a frog.

With the jar in hand, she carefully climbed back down and went to the counter. This was her job every Saturday — to fill the jars of candy in her aunt and uncle's sweetshop.

Her uncle paid her an allowance for doing so, though Libby didn't really have a choice in the matter. It was a family business, and as part of the family, she had to do her part.

When Libby had begun working at the (*very* part-time) job at the age of ten, Rebecca had been so envious. "Think of how many sweets you can eat," she'd said. "After all, you must sample one of everything to make sure you don't have a bad batch."

"You're joking, right?" Libby had said. "My uncle would be so upset if I ate that many. And even if he didn't mind, just think of the stomachache I'd get."

"But it would be the sweetest stomachache of your life," Rebecca had said.

Now Libby sighed as she put the jar back where it belonged. She couldn't deny it; she missed her bestie. But Rebecca seemed to be quite taken with her new group of friends, especially the ones who were boys.

The bell over the door jingled, as it always did when a customer walked in. With the jar in its rightful place, Libby returned to the counter as her uncle rushed out from the back room to offer assistance. Except it wasn't someone looking to buy candy. It was someone delivering flowers.

"Good afternoon," the delivery man said.

"Hello," Uncle Oliver replied as he ran his hand through his messy brown hair. "More flowers, I see."

"Yes." The delivery man handed Uncle Oliver the bouquet of red and white roses before he said, "I hope you enjoy them."

"Thank you," Uncle Oliver replied.

Libby's great-grandmother had passed away the week before. Many of the townsfolk in Tunbridge Wells, England knew Libby's family because of the candy store they owned: Mr. Pemberton's Olde Sweetshop. It was nice that people were thinking of them, Libby thought, but their house was beginning to look too much like a floral shop. Every day, her uncle brought the flowers home, since there wasn't room for them in their small place of business.

"I hope this is the last of them," Uncle Oliver said. "Is that terrible of me to say?"

"No, because I was thinking the same thing," Libby said.

Her uncle smiled. "It's very thoughtful of everyone. And kind. And we appreciate it, of course."

"Yes," Libby said. "Too bad people don't send something a little more useful, though."

"When your parents died all those years ago," he said as he set the bouquet down in a spot next to the register, "and you came to live with us, friends and acquaintances brought us meals. It was quite nice, although we didn't have much of an appetite for a time afterwards."

Libby didn't remember much from that time, since she'd been so young. "I know what you mean," she replied, walking out from behind the counter. "It's hard to eat when you're sad. The last morning at Camp Brookridge, before we all had to head for home, hardly anyone ate their breakfast."

The bell above the door jingled again, and this time, much to their relief, some customers strolled in. As Uncle Oliver walked over to greet the Thomason family, Libby started to sneak out, through the back. Her duties were done, and she was ready to go home. Libby and her uncle had an agreement that once the jars had been restocked, Libby could leave. But she heard Mrs. Thomason say something that made her stop and listen.

"Are you worried about the new sweetshop opening up soon?" Mrs. Thomason was asking her uncle.

"Not worried at all," Uncle Oliver replied with a smile.

"As you know, this shop has been in my family for fifty years, and no one knows sweets like we do. I am certain we will always have the best selection in town. Now, what may I help you with today?"

As he turned, he spotted Libby, and so she waved to let him know she was heading for home. Once outside, she hopped on her bike and pedaled, thinking about what her uncle had said.

Not worried at all.

She knew, from conversations her aunt and uncle had at home, that wasn't exactly true. Having another sweetshop fairly close by was pretty worrisome. Candy wasn't like produce; a person could go months without eating any. And now that there would be two shops in town, it could mean half the amount of business for the Pembertons.

Thankfully, their somewhat small town, which was quaint and charming and a wonderful place to live, did get a fair number of tourists every year. After all, there was much to see and do, with beautiful gardens and a few castles in the area to explore. People also came to visit the well-known Chalybeate Spring, discovered some four hundred years ago and, at one time, believed to miraculously cure people's illnesses.

But even with the tourists, it was hard to imagine that two sweetshops could really thrive in a town that wasn't especially large.

Libby recalled the time she'd tried to describe her English town to her three camp BFFs, Mia, Caitlin, and Hannah. They'd all been so curious about what it was like for Libby to live in England, since none of them had ever traveled outside of the States.

"It's quite lovely," she'd told them. "We're not very far from London, maybe sixty kilometers or so, and we're surrounded by gorgeous countryside. My uncle says we're fortunate to have some of England's best gardens nearby."

"What are the houses like?" Caitlin had asked Libby.

"We have many large, Victorian houses, but there are also lots of clapboard cottages too," Libby had said.

"I'm not really sure what any of that means," Mia had said, "but it sounds awesome!"

"The three of us should visit her one day," Hannah had said. "Wouldn't that be something, all of us in jolly old England?"

They'd all agreed it would be a lot of fun.

It only took Libby a few minutes to get home. When she

walked in the front door, the smell of freshly baked bread greeted her. Her aunt yelled, "Hi, Libby. I'm in the kitchen. Come see what the postman brought for you."

She couldn't get to the kitchen fast enough. Her aunt Jayne stood there wearing a cute green-and-blue apron, her curly brown hair pulled back with barrettes, as she held the package out in front of her. Libby clapped her hands together quickly before she grabbed it and read the name of the person who sent it.

"It's from Mia!" Libby cried, and took off for her room, her long ponytail swishing side to side as went. "I'd hoped it would be something from one of my summer camp friends."

"Everything go all right at the shop today?" her aunt called after her.

Libby stopped and turned around. "Yes. We got more flowers."

"Brilliant," Aunt Jayne said. "Just what we need. All right, go along and open your package. I can't wait to see what it is, when you feel like sharing."

"I can't wait either," Libby whispered as she closed her door.

Chapter 2

Gobstopper
different in the best way

Libby ripped open the package and jumped up and down when she found the charm bracelet. Once she got the initial excitement out of her system, she went to sit on her bed to study the charms. First, however, she had to move her great-grandma's journals out of the way. Her aunt had given them to her last week, thinking that Libby might like to look through them. And she did — they were fascinating to read.

With just the bracelet in front of her at last, Libby fingered the cute little flower charm. That had to be the one Caitlin had chosen, because someday Caitlin hoped to have her own flower shop. If only she could see all of the pretty arrangements in Libby's house right now. She'd love it.

Next, Libby admired the bird on the bracelet. That was Mia's. After all, Mia had written to Libby and told her about her bird-watching adventures with Lacy Bell, the teen actress she'd become friends with.

Libby hooked the bracelet around her wrist and a camp memory popped into her head. Caitlin, Mia, Libby, and Hannah stood at the edge of the dock, overlooking the lake.

"We're going to hold hands and jump in at the same time," Mia had said.

"Okay," Caitlin had replied as the four girls linked hands. "Jump really high. And kick your feet up behind you as we go. To make it more fun. On the count of three!"

"One, two, three!" they'd all counted, and on the word "three" they'd jumped into the cold water.

After they'd popped to the surface, they high-fived each other and then climbed back onto the dock and sat together, side by side, the sun warming their shivering bodies. Libby could remember feeling so happy in that moment. It was exactly as summer should be: full of sunshine, fun, and most of all, friendship.

She missed her friends. How easy it was with them. How

understanding they were, like with her aunt and uncle's strict rules regarding electronics. They'd all been so good about honoring their pact and writing letters to keep in touch, since Libby couldn't communicate with them any other way until she turned thirteen.

She read the letter Mia had sent along with the bracelet, and then pulled out a piece of paper to write her back.

Dear Mia,

The bracelet looks so cute with the charms you and Caitlin chose. Thank you for sending it to me! I will wear it every day and take very good care of it, I promise.

I'm sooooo happy your cast finally came off. What wonderful news! And I'm glad you and Lacy Bell are having fun together.

The bracelet came at a good time, not only because of the stuff going on with Rebecca and the new, competing sweetshop I told you will be opening, but also because my great-grandmother Grace passed away last week. It's been a pretty sad week, obviously.

I've been reading Grandma Grace's journals, and there's this jar I can't stop thinking about. She said when she was a child she had a friend, Mae, who moved to America with her family. When they were in their twenties, Mae decided to come and visit Grandma Grace here in England. She traveled on a ship (it was the 1940s) and she brought along a jar of homemade canned peaches as a gift. When Grandma Grace was writing this journal entry, one of the last ones she wrote, just a month or two ago, she talked about how she'd wanted to find that jar. See, Mae had written a short poem about friendship for Grace and they'd stuck it inside the jar after they'd eaten all the sweet, delicious peaches. Grandma Grace really wanted to read that poem again, but she couldn't find the jar. Isn't that sad?

She said for many, many years, she kept it on the windowsill in her kitchen. But she moved fifteen years ago, and she doesn't quite remember what happened to it after that. She said she often picked flowers from her garden and gave them to friends, using old jars or vases, and although she thought she would have been careful about that special jar, she must have been careless and given it away on accident. Three women's names are mentioned who might have it.

Mia, is it strange that I think I might want to try and find the jar? First of all, it's a wonderful symbol of friendship, but I also want to find it because I want to read the poem that meant so much to my great-grandma. I'm so curious about what it said. Now that I have the lucky bracelet, I feel like I can find Grandma Grace's jar if I try. Please, cross your fingers for me!

Well, time to say good-bye for now. I'm supposed to meet Cedric and Goldie at the park in a few minutes. You know how I told you about the boy I met a few weeks back, and how amazing it was that Dexter liked his dog? I forgot to tell you his name — it's Cedric.

Thanks again for sending the bracelet. Write again when you can!

Your Cabin 7 BFF,
Libby

Libby sealed up the letter, found her camp journal with her friends' addresses, and addressed the envelope to Mia. She returned to the kitchen as her aunt pulled out a loaf of bread from the oven.

"What did you get?" Aunt Jayne asked Libby.

"Remember I told you about the charm bracelet?" Libby said as she held out her wrist for her aunt to see. She set the letter on the counter, in a pile of mail waiting to be mailed.

"Isn't that lovely?" Aunt Jayne said.

While her aunt leaned in and examined the charms closely, Libby said, "I'm going to take Dexter for a walk now, if that's all right."

"Is it raining out?" Aunt Jayne asked as she turned back to the oven.

"Not right now," Libby said. "Just cool and cloudy."

"Make sure to wear a jacket," she called out, but Libby had already slipped her gray jacket on and was getting Dexter's leash from the basket where it was kept.

Dexter, a black Scottish terrier, and the cutest dog in the world as far as Libby was concerned, wagged his stubby little tail hard as Libby fastened the leash to his collar.

"Ready to go?" Libby asked Dexter, as she always did before they went. Dexter responded with a quick little *"Arf,"* and then the two were on their way.

As they walked toward the park, Libby thought about Cedric. He wasn't like most of the other boys at Bennett Memorial, the school she'd only recently begun attending. He was kind of shy and soft-spoken, and wasn't into rugby or cricket or any type of sport, really. It was hard for Libby to put her finger on what made Cedric different, exactly, just that he was. She was glad she and Dexter had met him and his dog, Goldie, for it gave her something to look forward to every Saturday, after she finished her work at the sweetshop.

When Dexter spotted Goldie across the park, he started pulling on the leash. His tail wagged so quickly, it seemed it might fly right off.

"Hold on there, boy," Libby said, smiling. "I'm walking as fast as I can."

When they finally reached them, the dogs greeted each other with some enthusiastic sniffs while Libby and Cedric exchanged hellos.

"I was beginning to think you'd forgotten," Cedric said.

"Am I late?" Libby asked. She bent down and gave Goldie, an adorable buff-colored cocker spaniel, a few pats.

"A little bit."

Libby stood up again and noticed that Cedric's short, red hair was quite messy today. It made her feel kind of bad, thinking of him rushing here, not even taking the time to comb his hair, so he would be on time. "Sorry. I had to open a package."

Cedric's green eyes grew big and round. "A package? Is it your birthday?"

Libby smiled. "No. A friend from summer camp sent me this bracelet." She held her arm out and pulled the sleeve of her jacket back so he could see it. "There are four of us who are taking turns wearing it."

"What if it gets lost in the mail?" Cedric asked.

Libby shrugged. Cedric did this sometimes — asked "what if" questions and seemed to be anxious about things. "It won't," she told him confidently.

"It could."

"So far it hasn't. We think it might be lucky, if you want to know the truth."

"Oh," he said. "I see. I have a lucky pair of trousers. They're my favorite. Obviously."

This is why she liked Cedric. A lucky pair of trousers? Most boys would probably think that sounded ridiculous. But not Cedric. The last time they'd met at the park to walk their dogs, Cedric had told her about his stamp collection, given to him by his grandfather. He'd said that sometimes he pretended the little stamps were pieces of artwork that his action figures liked to look at.

"I've never told anyone that before," he'd told Libby. "Please don't go spreading it around school."

She'd assured him she wouldn't. And in return, Libby had told him about her strange obsession with mermaids, and how a few years ago she had wanted her room painted blue like the sea and her headboard to be in the shape of a large seashell. She'd had so much fun turning her bedroom into an under-the-sea fantasy.

"I feel like I'm getting too old for the mermaid room," she'd said. "But I still like it. A lot."

"You should always do what makes you happy, I think," Cedric had said. And that was all that was said. They'd kept walking and talking like there was nothing different or strange about any of it.

And now, in the same manner, Cedric had told Libby without worry or embarrassment that he had a lucky pair of trousers. She couldn't wait to find out more.

Chapter 3

Sour Fizz Bomb
leaves a strange taste in your mouth

"What color are your lucky trousers?" Libby asked.

"Black."

"Black? That doesn't sound very exciting."

He narrowed his eyes and gave Libby a funny look. "I didn't say they were *exciting*. I said they were lucky."

That made Libby laugh. "Come on," she said. "Let's walk around the park so the dogs get their exercise."

"All right," he said as they started moving. "Are you hoping something lucky will happen today? Is that why you're wearing the bracelet?"

"Not really. I just like wearing it. Though I am hoping it will help me find a certain something that belonged to my great-grandma."

"The one who died?" Cedric asked.

"Yes," Libby said, feeling a little pinch in her heart at those words. She knew he didn't mean to be harsh or rude with the question. He just wanted to be clear about whom she was talking about.

"What do you want to find?" he asked as he picked a leaf off the ground and proceeded to crumble it in his hand. He then let the leafy brown confetti flutter to the ground.

"An old canning jar," Libby told him.

"And you thought black trousers weren't very exciting," he teased.

"I know, it sounds strange," Libby began to explain. "But I want to find it because a friend from America gave it to Grandma Grace, and wrote her a poem that she stuck inside. Grandma Grace thinks she accidentally gave the jar to one of her friends, along with some flowers. Haven't you ever had a certain something you wondered and wondered about? The jar with the poem is like that for me. I can't stop thinking about it."

"Well, I hope your lucky bracelet works," Cedric said as they stopped while Dexter and Goldie both sniffed a tree.

"My trousers have been lucky three different times. It's pretty amazing, really."

"Tell me about what happened," Libby said as they started walking again.

"The first time I wore them, I found a pound on the pavement. The second time I wore them, my parents learned they'd been approved by the bank to open up the sweetshop. And finally, I met you and Dexter at this very park while wearing them."

Libby knew she should say something about the third thing he mentioned. That it was nice of him to think of the day the two of them had met as a lucky day. But she'd stopped in her tracks as soon as he'd said the word, "sweetshop."

It couldn't be, could it?

The two hadn't known each other very long. And in the short amount of time they'd been friends, they hadn't talked much about their families at all. Cedric had no idea that Libby's family owned Mr. Pemberton's Olde Sweetshop. He didn't know her parents had died when she was four and she'd gone to live with her mother's brother and his wife. Libby had a different last name from her aunt and uncle, because her father hadn't been a Pemberton, only her mother. Because of all this, it wasn't something Cedric would have easily put together.

"Libby?" Cedric asked. "Are you all right? Did I say the wrong thing? I mean, did that embarrass you?"

She shook her head. "No. Not at all. I'm glad we met too. I'm just, well, I'm curious what you meant, about opening a sweetshop."

Cedric smiled. "Oh, I see. You love sweets then, is that it? Me too. Which is why I'm so excited we'll be opening up The Sweet Retreat very soon. Don't you love that name? My mum thought of it. We knew we wanted a name that sounded new and fun, not old and stuffy like that other shop in town. Anyway, it's been my parents' dream forever to have a business all their own. My dad lost his job recently and they decided it was finally time for them to follow their dream. My mum has very fond memories of a sweetshop she visited as a child, and that's why they chose to sell candy. She wants to give other children happy memories like the ones she has."

For a moment, it felt like someone had punched Libby in the stomach. She held her breath as she tried to decide what to do. Should she tell him? Tell him that the "old and stuffy" sweetshop belonged to her family? But if she told him, surely he wouldn't like her very much anymore. Would he?

Libby scanned the park as she tried to decide whether or not to tell Cedric they were now sweetshop competitors. That's when she spotted Rebecca, on the other side of the park, talking and laughing with her new group of friends. She looked so happy, and Libby knew she should probably be glad about that, but all it did was make her miss her best friend even more.

Seeing Rebecca and feeling the hurt all over again made her want to hold tightly to everything else she didn't want to lose. She couldn't tell Cedric. Not yet, anyway. She had to find a way to break it to him gently. To make sure he knew that it didn't matter to her, and she really didn't want it to bother him, either. When she told him, she had to know for sure that they could still be friends.

Libby turned around and took off in the opposite direction of Rebecca. "Come on," she told Cedric. "Let's go this way instead."

"Are you all right?" Cedric asked. "You're acting sort of strange."

"I just spotted my best friend over there. Or, the person who *used* to be my best friend, I'm not really sure. I haven't spoken to her in a while, and I miss her." She looked at Cedric and tried to smile. "It hurts, you know?"

He nodded. "I'm sorry. She doesn't go to Bennett Memorial like us, then?"

"No," Libby said. "I'd hoped that wouldn't matter. I mean, it shouldn't matter."

Just like it shouldn't matter that Cedric's parents were seen as enemies in Libby's home, for potentially hurting their family business.

Why do these things have to be so complicated? Libby thought to herself. She looked down at the charm bracelet she wore and thought of her time at camp with Mia, Caitlin, and Hannah. That was how friendship should be. Fun and easy, and filled with happy memories, like the one at the lake.

And then, she found herself missing them too, as tears welled up in her eyes.

"We need to cheer you up," Cedric said, looking over at her. "I've never seen a walk in the park make someone so sad. I wish The Sweet Retreat were already open so I could take you there. I'd let you pick out any sweets you'd like. That'd make you happy, wouldn't it?"

She thought of all the work she'd done earlier, filling up the jars at the shop. If only he knew that seeing more candy today was about the last thing she wanted to do.

Libby couldn't help but laugh at how silly the whole thing was.

"What?" Cedric asked.

"It's just, my stomach kind of hurts, and candy doesn't really sound that good right now," she said. "But it's very sweet. I mean, you're sweet. Candy is too, of course, but I meant . . . oh, never mind."

Cedric laughed. And Libby realized she felt a little better. At least, she would until the next time Cedric decided to mention The Sweet Retreat.

Chapter 4

Rainbow Drop
like eating a colorful, well-kept secret

"Let's sit on that bench," Cedric said, pointing. "I brought something I want to show you. Something I've been working on."

Before they sat down, Cedric pulled some papers out of the pocket of his jacket. He reached over and handed them to Libby. As he did, she gave Dexter's leash to Cedric so she could have her hands free. While Libby and Cedric settled in on the bench, the two dogs lay down next to each other on the grass, perfectly content.

The pages Cedric had given to Libby were filled with drawings, and words here and there. And they were folded to be like a book. A comic book, Libby realized.

"You made this?" Libby asked.

"Yes."

Libby read the first words of the story out loud. "When he was a young boy, Vincent Rooper lost his parents in a terrible accident at sea. At least, everyone thought it was an accident. Everyone but Vincent, who knew the truth — but refused to talk about what had happened that dreadful day. Losing his parents wasn't the only thing that had happened at sea. And every month that a blue moon occurred, he was reminded of the tragic day, for Vincent Rooper disappeared. And in his place, Lobsterman appeared."

Cedric had drawn Lobsterman to be a big man with huge claws for hands.

"You're a really good artist," Libby said. "But is Lobsterman a good guy or a bad guy?"

"He defeats the villains, so he's a good guy."

Libby nodded. "I love making art too. But I like drawing nature. Trees and flowers. That sort of thing. So, I guess you like reading comic books too, right?"

Cedric took his pages back and handed Dexter's leash back to Libby. "Yep. They're one of my favorite things. What do you like to read?"

"Stories about friendship, mostly. Animals too. But you

know what? My friend Caitlin, who I met at camp, brought a little book of poetry along with her and we took turns reading from it. I really liked the poetry. More than I thought I would. Maybe that's why I want to find the jar and poem that my grandma Grace talked about in her journal. I don't know. This situation with Rebecca just really bothers me, and I keep thinking maybe the poem will help me somehow."

After the last words were out, Libby wondered if maybe she'd shared too much. She didn't want to scare Cedric off with her friendship drama. And yet, she couldn't help but feel a little bit better about finally telling someone that there were troubles between her and Rebecca.

Cedric leaned forward and untangled Goldie's leash, which had managed to get wrapped around Dexter's. "Would you like me to go with you? To talk to the ladies about the jar?"

Libby thought about this for a minute before she responded. In some ways, it would be nice to have someone along with her. She couldn't deny that she was a little bit nervous about asking these women about a jar they might not even have. But on the other hand, what if they mentioned Mr. Pemberton's? It came up often in conversations with other people. Libby would feel horrible if Cedric found out like that rather than her telling him. And she knew she would have to tell him, eventually. She just needed time to figure out the best way to do it.

"No," Libby said, leaning back against the bench. "I think it's something I need to do on my own."

"What if they slam the door in your face? Or call you names? What will you do if something bad happens?"

Once again, Cedric was thinking of the worst possible scenarios. "Why would they slam the door in my face? It's not like I'm trying to sell them something like that ridiculous magic carpet cleaner everyone's talking about."

"Some people just don't like to be bothered," Cedric said.

Was he right? Would the people be irritated with her for knocking on their door and asking about a silly old jar they might not even have?

"If I don't look for it," Libby said, thinking out loud, "I think I might regret it for the rest of my life. Maybe that sounds overly dramatic or whatever, but it's like a puzzle that's been put in front of me and it's my job to find the missing pieces."

"I like puzzles," Cedric said.

"Or maybe it's more of a mystery," Libby said. "I don't know. All I know is I want to find that jar with the poem."

"When will you start looking?"

"Tomorrow," Libby said. "Now that my lucky bracelet has arrived, there's nothing else getting in my way."

Cedric rose from the bench. "I should get home. Come find me at school on Monday. I want to know what happens tomorrow."

Libby stood up. "All right. I hope I have good news."

"Me too." He looked at her. "Would you like to borrow my lucky trousers before you go knocking on doors?"

Libby smiled. "No thanks. Like I said, I have my brace-let. Besides, you should keep all of the luck for yourself. You never know when you might need some again."

"Well, I don't mind sharing. If you change your mind, give me a ring."

Libby waved as she turned in the opposite direction. "I'll see you on Monday."

Cedric waved back.

As Libby and Dexter walked toward home, she thought about The Sweet Retreat and what her aunt and uncle would say if she told them she'd become friends with the owners' son. Would they forbid her from seeing him? She couldn't be sure what they would say, really, so it was probably best not to mention it to them.

How strange that her normally boring life was now filled with mysteries and secrets. Some might think the whole thing was exciting, but to Libby, it seemed mostly overwhelming.

Chapter 5

Chocolate Truffle
don't get caught eating too many

After lunch on Sunday, Libby rode her bicycle to Margaret's house, the first friend her grandma had mentioned in her journal. Margaret had been one of Grandma Grace's best friends, and Libby knew her well. When Libby had told her aunt and uncle that morning that she wanted to go and visit Margaret, and see how she was doing, they both thought it was very thoughtful and kind.

Of course, it wasn't the complete and honest truth, but it was true, in a way. She liked Margaret, for a couple of different reasons. First of all, Margaret always had the best biscuits to serve to company who came to visit. Not only that, she had a teacup collection Libby adored, many of them passed down through generations.

When she reached Margaret's cottage, she parked her bike and made her way to the purple front door, rubbing the charm bracelet for luck. When Libby had been younger, she'd been fascinated by that door. She'd even asked Margaret why she had a purple door and Margaret's answer had simply been, "Well, why not? It's a lovely door, isn't it?"

Now, Libby knocked, hoping her great-grandma's friend would be happy to see her.

"Libby!" Margaret exclaimed when she opened the door. She peered at the young girl over her reading glasses. "This is quite the surprise. Please, come in."

Margaret was a short, stocky woman who rarely smiled but had a friendly face all the same. She slipped the reading glasses off as Libby made her way into the small house.

"I hope it's all right that I stopped by," Libby said. "I just wanted to come over and say hello. See how you're doing."

"Well, isn't that nice of you," Margaret replied. "Come into the kitchen and take a seat. I'll make us a spot of tea, how's that sound?"

"That sounds nice, thanks."

Libby followed Margaret into the cozy kitchen, which was bright and cheerful, with walls the color of lemons, and her pretty teacups displayed in a cabinet in the far corner, near the kitchen table.

"I've added some cups to my collection," Margaret said as she put the kettle on the stove and turned it on. "Would you like to see them?"

"I'd love to," Libby said, sitting down at the table.

Margaret went to the cabinet and pulled down two teacups along with their saucers. One of them was covered in lavender roses, while the other one was mint green and white with three four-leaf clovers on the inside of the cup. Gold lettering on the saucer read, "Good luck."

"They're both pretty, but I like this one," Libby said as she examined the four-leaf clovers. "It's very different."

"And supposedly lucky," Margaret said. "You can drink your tea out of that one, then."

Margaret picked up the teacups and took them to the counter, next to the stove. "I know it's early and you probably just finished lunch, but would you like a biscuit with your tea?"

Libby smiled. "Yes, please."

As Margaret fiddled with the tea and biscuits, Libby tried to get up the nerve to ask about the jar. She wanted to get it out of the way. The sooner, the better, her aunt always said.

Just as she was about to ask, the telephone rang, in another room. Margaret turned to Libby and said, "Let me get that, then we'll have our tea."

"That's fine," Libby said. "Take your time."

It seemed like maybe this was the lucky break Libby needed. Perhaps she could simply look for the jar on her own, and not even mention it to Margaret. If she found it, she could grab the poem from the jar and just slip it into her pocket. Margaret would never have to know.

Libby hopped up and began quietly opening cupboard doors. She could hear Margaret talking in the other room. As long as Margaret kept talking, Libby knew she was probably safe from being caught. Still, that knowledge didn't stop Libby's legs from trembling. It would be so embarrassing if Margaret found her peering into her cupboards.

Libby had searched every cupboard but the ones she was too short to reach. As she looked around for a step stool, she heard Margaret say good-bye, so she quickly ran back to the table, sitting down just in the knick of time.

"Did I hear you get up?" Margaret asked as she went to the stove.

Had she seen Libby snooping? Did she know? Libby swallowed hard. "Oh er, yes, I was just washing my hands."

"Oh, good," Margaret said. "Our tea is ready."

As the older woman went to work pouring hot water and arranging the biscuits on a plate, Libby decided it was now or never.

"One of the reasons I came here is so I could ask you something," Libby said. "About my grandma Grace. If you don't mind?"

"No, I don't mind at all," Margaret replied matter-of-factly. "Ask away."

Libby spoke slowly, choosing her words carefully. "She mentioned an old, clear canning jar that her friend Mae brought over from America in the forties. She was looking for it shortly before she died, because it was special to her, and she couldn't find it. I wondered if she might have given it to you, with some flowers in it? I know she often gave you and some of her other friends flowers from her pretty garden."

Margaret pulled out a wooden stool that sat in the corner

and said, "If you'd like, you can come and look for yourself. I keep all of my vases and whatnot in the cupboard above the sink."

Libby stood up, her legs slightly wobbly again, but this time for a different reason. Margaret was letting her look for the jar. It almost seemed too good to be true. Maybe she'd actually find it.

Libby climbed the stool and peered into the cupboard that was filled with vases and jars. There were so many. She picked up one, and then another, and then another.

They seemed to be never-ending. How would she ever find it?

"Can I help you there?" Margaret asked as she took the tea tray to the table.

"I think I might have to take them all out so I can see them. Would that be all right?"

"Of course. Why don't you hand them to me, and I'll set them here, on the counter. It will go quickly that way."

So that's what they did, and Margaret had been right. It did go quickly. And because Margaret was a smart lady, she sorted the items as they went. Vases and colored jars were in one spot while clear jars were put in another.

Libby stepped down off the stool and took everything in. There were only five clear jars, and none of them really looked like jars you'd put peaches in. They were too small — more like jelly jars.

"She said the jar wasn't anything special," Libby said, picking up one of the small jars and examining it. "Just a clear, old Mason jar. But it didn't matter what it looked like; it was special to her for other reasons." Libby looked at Margaret. "That's exactly what she said."

"I'm sorry it doesn't appear to be here," Margaret said. "Are there other friends of hers you can check with?"

"Yes," Libby said as she leaned back against the counter. "Franny and Eloise were also mentioned. I guess I'll have to see if one of them has it."

"Well, let's sit down and have our tea, shall we?" Margaret said. "I think you'll like the biscuits I made yesterday. Light and buttery with a hint of cinnamon."

"Did you know they call them c
Libby asked as she returned to th
mer camp told me that in A

"Oh yes," Margaret said
I traveled there a number

Margaret began to tell a story, but Libby wasn't listening. She was staring at the words "Good luck" on the saucer.

She took a sip of her tea. It didn't taste lucky at all. In fact, it tasted a lot like disappointment.

Chapter 6

Chocolate Rose Cream
makes everything rosy

After a few months at Bennett Memorial, her new school, Libby finally felt somewhat at home there. She'd gotten used to wearing the school uniform, which consisted of a kilt, a white blouse, and a Bennett blazer. She'd even grown comfortable with being around much older students (mostly, she just chose to ignore them). Some of her classes were pretty challenging, but she liked all of her teachers, so that made them tolerable. For the most part.

On Monday, Libby found Cedric during lunchtime, like he'd asked her to do. Normally he ate with his best friend, Louis, but today he sat by himself.

"Hi," Libby said. "Where's Louis?"

"He's at home, sick," Cedric said as he munched on an

apple. "Do you want to sit with me, instead of the group of girls you usually eat with?"

"Okay. Sure."

"Did you find the jar you were looking for?"

Libby sighed as she set her tray down, before she plopped down in the seat across from Cedric. "No. She only had five clear jars and none of them were the type I'm looking for."

Cedric shook his head. "You should have worn my lucky trousers."

It made Libby smile. "They wouldn't have helped, since she doesn't have the jar. So now I have to visit Franny. I think I'm going to do it this weekend sometime. But the thing is, I don't know Franny very well. She was a neighbor of Grandma Grace's, but we never visited her the way we visited Margaret. Maybe they weren't really friends, just people who lived next door to each other."

"What if she didn't even like your grandma?" Cedric asked. "That would be really awkward for you."

"But Grandma Grace was a nice lady. I think everyone who knew her liked her. Besides, if she gave flowers to Franny, that must mean they were friendly with each other."

"I suppose," Cedric said as he set down his apple core. "Hey, the grand opening of The Sweet Retreat is on Saturday. Do you think you and your family could come? I know it'd mean a lot to my parents. They're really nervous about the whole thing."

Libby looked down at the table, her mind frantically trying to come up with an excuse. Finally she decided it might be best to keep her answer vague. "I can probably come. I don't know about my family, though. I'll have to check."

"All right," he said. "To be honest, I'm not that excited about it. Louis invited me to go with him and his dad to Kent Comics. It's a comic book shop over in Orpington. I really want to go, but my parents said I have to be at the sweetshop *all* day long."

Libby wasn't sure what to say to that, so she simply said, "Sorry."

"It won't be so bad if you come and keep me company for a while," Cedric replied. "I bet my dad will let us sample some of the sweets. Have you ever heard of chocolate frogs?"

Libby knew he was hoping to get some weird reaction out of her. But the words *chocolate frogs* just made her feel even more anxious about the big secret she was keeping from him. "Yes," she said. "I've heard of them. They're Rebecca's favorite, actually."

"Oh," Cedric said. "Sorry. Sore subject. Maybe you could ask her to come along with you? Buy her some chocolate frogs and patch things up between the two of you."

"I don't think so," Libby said as she picked at her shepherd's pie. "I mean, I feel like what's going on between us is too big for chocolate frogs. I don't even know what it is that's going on, exactly. That's what's strange. Things are just . . . different between us. She's changed. Or maybe I have. I'm not sure."

"How can anything be too big for chocolate?" he said. "Chocolate makes anything better. Doesn't it?"

"I wish," she said.

"Yeah," he said. "Me too. Then I could just make sure my mum and dad had lots of chocolate on Saturday, and I could go along with Louis to the comic book store."

"You really do like comic books a lot, don't you?" she asked.

"Yes. I might like them even more than sweets," he said as he reached into his lunch bag and pulled out two chocolate truffles. "If you can believe that."

"Why do you like them so much?" she asked. "Comic books, I mean?"

"I think it's because the story comes to life in such a unique way because of the artwork. I can see the story really clearly in my head. And the stories are really exciting, with lots of action. I like that."

"Is that what you want to do when you grow up? Write and draw comic books?"

"I think so. If I'm good enough."

Libby didn't know what she wanted to do when she grew up. Her aunt and uncle often talked about her taking over Mr. Pemberton's Olde Sweetshop someday. She'd told them that would be awfully weird, since her last name wasn't Pemberton like all the other owners of the shop. They said it didn't matter. Maybe not, but what did matter was that Libby thought working at the sweetshop the rest of her life sounded completely boring.

Of course, now, with a second shop in town, who knew what might happen. What if The Sweet Retreat put Mr. Pemberton's out of business?

"Are you all right?" Cedric asked Libby. "You look a little pale."

"I just had a terrible thought about something," Libby said. "It's too terrible to even talk about. Sorry."

"That's all right," Cedric said. He passed one of the truffles across the table. "Here. This should make you feel better."

Libby popped it into her mouth. The delicious chocolate melted in her mouth and she let herself enjoy it for a moment.

"Do you feel better?" Cedric asked her.

She smiled. "I do."

Cedric threw his hands in the air, a big grin on his face. "See? What did I tell you? Chocolate is the solution to everything."

If only, Libby thought.

Chapter 7

Cherry BonBon
friends will fight over this one

When Libby got home from school, Dexter was sitting on the chair by the front window, watching for her, like he did every day. She walked in and Dexter jumped from the chair and ran over to her, dancing around to let her know how happy he was to see her.

"Come on," she said. "You want a treat?" This was another phrase Dexter understood completely.

"Hi, Lib," Aunt Jayne said when Libby walked into the kitchen. "How was school today?"

"Fine, I guess," Libby said as she got a treat out of the box. She threw it across the floor and watched Dexter chase after it.

"You don't sound very convincing about that," her aunt said.

Libby couldn't stop thinking about the grand opening on Saturday. She'd told Cedric she would come, and there didn't seem to be any way to get out of it now. Unless she pretended to be sick, and she didn't like the idea of going that far.

Dexter took off toward the entryway, due to the sound of the front door clicking open and then closed. Libby looked at her aunt, confused, since her uncle didn't usually get home this early. Aunt Jayne gave her a little shrug, indicating her confusion as well.

"Oliver?" Aunt Jayne called. "Is that you?"

"Yes," he replied. A second later, he appeared in the doorway of the kitchen. "I closed the shop early today. I'm not feeling very well."

Aunt Jayne scowled. "Oh no. What's wrong?"

"Horrible headache," he replied. "Think I'll go lie down for a while."

"You should take some aspirin first," Aunt Jayne said. She hurried to the sink and filled a glass with water. Then she went to the cupboard and pulled out a bottle of pills.

"You know, we have to do something," Uncle Oliver said, leaning up against the doorframe. He looked really tired to Libby. And maybe a little bit sad.

His wife gave him a funny look. "We *are* doing something. You're going to take these pills —"

"No. I don't mean that," he said. "I mean, about the grand opening on Saturday. We can't let them walk all over us."

She handed him the water and pills and said, "Don't worry about that now. Go lie down." She glanced over at Libby, a concerned look on her face. "We'll discuss it later."

After Uncle Oliver swallowed the pills, he handed the empty glass back to his wife. "Time is running out," he said. "We simply must figure out what we're going to do about this."

Libby could practically taste the tension in the room. She couldn't remember a time when her uncle seemed as stressed as he did right now.

"Maybe we should have a sale," Libby said, trying to sound cheerful. "A really big sale. Like, the biggest sale we've ever had. Make the candy so cheap, there's no question as to which sweetshop they should visit that day."

Aunt Jayne crossed her arms and smiled. "Yes, we've talked about a sale. The problem is a grand opening sounds so exciting. It's hard to compete with that. We need a name or a phrase that makes people really sit up and take notice."

"That's easy," Libby said.

Her uncle chuckled. "It is? Well, please, do tell."

"The shop's been around for fifty years, so call it a fiftieth anniversary sale. And give everyone a fifty percent discount."

He groaned. "Fifty percent? I'm not sure we can —"

"Oliver, I think it's a brilliant idea," Aunt Jayne said. "What a wonderful way to remind the community of our history. And to celebrate that as well."

Uncle Oliver reached back and scratched his head, something he seemed to do when he was lost in thought. Finally he said, "You know, you're right. Both of you. We *should* celebrate being in business for fifty years. It's a big deal. I'd have to get an e-mail sent out to our mailing list tonight. And update our website. I don't know if there's time to run an advertisement in the paper. Jayne, would you mind giving them a ring?"

"Of course," Aunt Jayne replied.

"I could make posters to hang in the shop windows," Libby suggested. "On bright, colorful paper."

"Perfect," Uncle Oliver said. "I'll need both of you to work on Saturday, for the entire time we're open. Is that all right with the two of you?"

Now Libby'd done it. She'd gotten herself backed into a corner with no way out. How could she go to the grand opening of The Sweet Retreat if she had to work all day? And what would she tell Cedric when she didn't show up like she'd promised she would?

"Mr. Pemberton's belongs to all of us," Aunt Jayne said as she put her arm around her husband. "Your problems are our problems, and we'll help any way we can. Right, Lib?"

She was so anxious thinking about Saturday, that Libby's mouth felt as dry as sandpaper. "Right," she managed to say as she went to the sink to get herself a drink of water.

"Oh," Aunt Jayne said. "Libby, I'm so sorry, I almost forgot. A letter came for you today. It's there, on the counter."

"Think I'll take it to my room," Libby said after she picked it up and read that it was from her camp friend Hannah.

"Thanks for the encouragement and ideas, love," Libby's uncle said to her. "I feel much better now that we have a plan. Do you have time to do the posters tonight, so I can hang them in the windows tomorrow?"

"Yes," she replied. "I'll do them after I finish my homework."

Both her aunt and uncle smiled at her as she turned to leave. She wished she could feel as relieved as they looked. It felt a bit like two countries about to go to war, while she was stuck in the middle, trying to keep the peace.

When she got to her room, she plopped down on her bed and read Hannah's letter.

Dear Libby,

Happy almost Thanksgiving! Wait, why am I saying that? People in England don't celebrate Thanksgiving, right? Okay, forget I ever said anything. Thanksgiving is a big deal to my family. My daddy would probably say it's because we have a lot to be thankful for, even though I think he just says that since that's what you're supposed to say. Between you and me, I think it's because we all really like to eat. My grandma always makes my favorite kind of pie — banana cream. Yum! I'm telling ya, I love banana cream pie the way a grizzly bear loves fish. I'd eat it every day if I could. Great, now I have pie on the brain, which is not very fun when I have to wait over a week to eat some.

Last time you wrote to me, you said things were strange between you and your best friend, Rebecca. I hope by now things have gotten better between you. I know with one of my friends, when something isn't right between us, I try to lighten the mood with a joke. Or even a silly prank. Something to make her laugh, you know? Like my daddy always says, laughter is the best medicine.

Do you ever wonder what it would be like if you, me, Caitlin, and Mia all lived in the same neighborhood and went to the same school? Wouldn't that be awesome? I can't wait to see you all again next summer. I think on January first, we should start counting down the days.

Right now, I'm counting down the days until Christmas. I think something BIG is going to happen. I overheard my parents talking, and although I didn't hear everything they said, it sounded like they are finally, FINALLY going to get me my own horse. Isn't that exciting? I've wanted my own horse since I was like five years old. I'm already thinking about names. Hopefully this will be the best Christmas ever.

Please write me back and tell me what's happening over there in jolly old England. I miss you! And I will eat lots of pie for you on Thanksgiving, don't you worry about that.

Your Cabin 7 BFF,

Hannah

As she folded up the letter, Libby realized she'd had a grin on her face the entire time she'd been reading. Not only that, for approximately one minute and twenty-seven seconds, she had forgotten about the sweetshop war and the missing jar.

That was why camp had been so fun. Good friends, good times, and no real life to worry about. She reached over to her nightstand and grabbed her camp journal. She turned the pages until she found the one she was looking for.

Q of the Day: If you were stranded on a desert island, what's the one object you'd want to have with you?

One object? That would have to be a freezer, filled with my grandma's pies. She makes the best pies! Don't

even try to tell me that a freezer full of pies
doesn't count as one object, because it totally does.
Just like an apple tree filled with apples is one object.
Right?
  Your Cabin 7 BFF,
  Hannah

Libby had laughed when she first read it, and she laughed
again now. The best medicine, for sure.

Chapter 8

Gummy Worm
funny, or just strange?

$\mathscr{B}$ennett Memorial was a bit too far from home for Libby to ride her bike, so Aunt Jayne took turns giving rides with three other parents. But on Thursday, she told Libby she'd pick her up after school and take her shopping for some new shoes, which she desperately needed.

Libby ended up getting two pairs, since the store was having a sale. The school uniform rules were very clear — girls had to wear black shoes with no more than a one-inch heel. She'd chosen some super cute Mary Janes for school and blue-and-neon-pink Nike trainers for other times. She was most excited about the new trainers, since they'd be perfect for walks in the park with Dexter.

Once they were back in the car, Aunt Jayne said, "Before

we head home, I need to stop at the pet store right around the corner here. Dexter's just about out of food."

"Can I pick out a new toy for him?" Libby asked. "Or a bone. Something? Sometimes I worry that he must be bored."

"Well, a dog's life isn't particularly exciting, is it?"

"That's why I like taking him on walks," Libby said. "Dogs deserve to have fun too."

Her aunt laughed. "I suppose that's true."

Libby cleared her throat as she realized this was the perfect opportunity to bring up the dilemma she had about Saturday, without actually discussing the *real* dilemma. "So would it be all right if I took a break on Saturday, during the anniversary sale, so I could take Dexter for a walk? He's gotten quite used to going for a long one with me on Saturdays. I'd hate to disappoint him."

Aunt Jayne turned into the parking lot of the pet store. "I think we'll have to wait and see how things go. If it's terribly busy, like we hope it will be, we'll need you to be climbing that ladder for us, helping to get the jars down while we weigh the sweets and complete the transactions."

"But if things slow down at some point, then I can go?" Libby asked as her aunt parked the car.

"I think that would probably be fine," Jayne said.

As they walked into the pet store, Libby breathed a little easier, knowing she at least had a chance now to get away. Hopefully it wouldn't be super busy the entire day.

"I'll get the food," Aunt Jayne said. "And you go pick out a toy for him. I'll meet you at the register."

"All right," Libby said before they turned in opposite directions.

As she passed the cat food aisle, a girl about her age practically knocked her over, coming around the corner. It happened fast, and it took a moment for Libby to realize she knew this girl.

Rebecca.

"Sorry," Rebecca said. "I didn't see you there."

"That's okay," Libby said. She pointed to the cat food in Rebecca's hand. "How's Marvin doing anyway? I haven't seen him, you know, in a while."

After she said it, Libby realized how ridiculous that sounded. She could feel her cheeks getting warm.

Rebecca tossed her brown hair back. "Oh, he's fine. Still sleeps about twenty-three hours a day. Must be nice, right?"

"Yeah," is all Libby could manage to say. Why did this

have to be so awkward? She didn't want to talk about Marvin. She wanted to talk about the two of them. About what had happened. About how much she missed Rebecca and how she wished things could go back to the way they used to be, before summer camp and before Rebecca had met her new friends. But no words came. Libby remembered what Hannah had said in her letter: *Laughter is the best medicine.*

The problem was that it's hard to be funny when all you feel is worry and tension. Still, she decided she had to try.

"Sometimes I think if cats and dogs could talk," Libby said, "it'd really surprise us what they might say. Like I bet Dexter would be happy about everything. 'Time to eat — yay! Time to go for a walk — double yay! A treat — oh boy!' And if Marvin could talk, he'd probably say, 'Please, just leave me alone, all right? You people annoy me. All I want is a little peace and quiet!'"

Rebecca grimaced. "What? Marvin would not say that. I don't annoy him. He loves me, Libby. You make him sound like an old, grumpy cat, and he's not like that at all."

Libby wanted to turn and run the other way. What had she done? "No, I know, I was just trying to be funny. Because cats and dogs are so different. I didn't mean anything by it. Honest."

"I gotta go," Rebecca said with a sigh. "My mum and little brother are in the car, waiting for me."

"Please don't be mad. Please? The last thing I want is for us to fight like cats and dogs because of my bad joke." Libby waited for Rebecca to smile. She didn't. "Rebecca, I wanted you to laugh. Remember how much fun we used to have together? I want it to be like that again. That's all."

"I really gotta go. Bye."

Rebecca scurried away so fast, Libby couldn't even return the good-bye.

Feeling totally defeated, Libby made her way to the dog toy aisle and tried to focus on figuring out what Dexter might like to play with, but all she could think about was the way Rebecca had looked at her after she'd tried to be funny. Like she was the meanest, most horrible person on the planet.

"What's taking so long?" It was her aunt. Libby had been so busy trying to focus on the toys, she hadn't seen her walk up.

"Sorry," Libby said, trying not to cry. "I'm just having a bit of . . . trouble."

"Well, here," Aunt Jayne replied. "Let me help you." She reached up and grabbed a stuffed cat off the rack. It squeaked when she squeezed it. Just what Libby needed, a constant reminder of the dog-and-cat joke that probably ruined her friendship with Rebecca forever.

"Anything but that one," Libby pleaded.

"Yes, I see how that could get annoying after a while," Aunt Jayne said as she put the cat back in its place. "How about a new rope, for playing tug-of-war? You know how he loves playing that."

Libby nodded her head in agreement. It seemed fitting, for just about everything in her life right now felt like a tug-of-war, and now she'd actually be playing it for real with the dog.

How perfect.

Chapter 9

Chocolate Pecan Cluster
worth Standing in line for

When Oliver, Jayne, and Libby arrived at the sweetshop Saturday morning, there were already some customers standing outside, waiting to get in.

Uncle Oliver smiled as he said, "Just give us a few minutes to get things in order, and then we'll be open for business."

"I can't believe people are already here. That's a good sign, yes?" Aunt Jayne said after they'd gotten inside and closed the door.

Uncle Oliver smiled. "A very good sign." He turned to Libby. "Thanks again for the brilliant idea of an anniversary sale, sweetheart."

"You're welcome," Libby replied.

Her uncle walked over to the register with the envelope of change he'd gotten from the bank the day before. "All right. Let's get to work," he said. "Libby, there are a few jars that are in desperate need of filling. I made a list yesterday and it's there, on the counter, near where you're standing. While you do that, I'm going to put this change in the register. Jayne, would you mind giving the counters a quick wipe down?"

"Certainly." And with that, they were off and running.

Once the doors opened, business was steady for the first few hours. When lunchtime arrived, they took turns eating sandwiches that Aunt Jayne had brought from home in the back room. As Libby ate her lunch, she recalled running into Cedric at school the day before and how he'd asked her again if she would stop by The Sweet Retreat to see the place and say hello. She'd planned to tell him something had come up and she wouldn't be able to come after all. But as he looked at her and pleaded with her to come and see the shop, she couldn't do it. She couldn't lie to him. She already felt guilty enough because she was keeping her family's business a secret from him.

After she wolfed down her tomato-and-cheese sandwich,

Libby returned to work to find the shop empty for the first time all day. She knew this was her one and only chance. The Sweet Retreat was across town, but on her bike, she figured she could make it in twenty minutes or so. She'd go in, say hello to Cedric, and only stay for a few minutes before she'd head back to the shop.

"Is it all right if I take a break and go home and take Dexter for a walk?" Libby asked. "He likes to walk around the park a couple of times, so I'll probably be gone about an hour."

She'd barely gotten the words out when some customers walked through the door. She held her breath, hoping this didn't mean the answer would be no.

Uncle Oliver greeted the people, so Libby walked over to her aunt. "Please? May I go?"

And then, another group of customers came in. And behind them, an even bigger group. Libby's heart sunk. She knew she was now stuck here for good.

Her aunt gave her a sympathetic look. "I'm sorry. All hands on deck, I'm afraid."

"Libby," her uncle called. "Can you please get me the jar of sour strawberry bites?"

And so it went, for the rest of the afternoon.

At five, Uncle Oliver put the "Closed" sign in the window and then danced a silly little jig across the shop. "I can't believe how much business we did today," he said.

"Hopefully everyone was here and not at the other place," Aunt Jayne said. Libby had noticed they never called the other shop by its name, as if it were evil. Like "He-Who-Must-Not-Be-Named" in the Harry Potter books.

Libby was glad the sale had been so successful, but there was a part of her that felt bad for Cedric and his family. She didn't want their business to completely fail. That would be horrible.

"I think we should drive by the other place and see what's going on," Uncle Oliver said. "I saw that they were staying open until seven tonight."

Libby felt panic rising up. What if Cedric saw them driving by, but not stopping to go in? What would she tell him? She looked outside and realized it would be dark soon, and that made her feel better.

"Why not take it a step further?" Aunt Jayne asked. "Let's go inside. Introduce ourselves. Tell them there are no hard feelings and we wish them the very best."

"No!" Libby shouted, before she had the good sense to stop herself.

Both her aunt and uncle stared at her.

"I mean, I don't want to do that. It would be so embarrassing. Like, what are they going to say back to us? What if they don't feel the same way?"

Uncle Oliver scratched the back of his head, thinking. Libby rubbed her bracelet, hoping for some luck to come her way. They couldn't go into The Sweet Retreat. They just couldn't.

Finally, her uncle said, "Today's their big day. I don't want to intrude on that if we're not really welcome, and we don't know if we are or not. We certainly wouldn't be stopping in to buy anything, so it does feel a bit wrong."

Libby let out the breath she'd been holding. "Exactly."

"But I still want to drive by," Uncle Oliver said. "There's no harm in that, right? And after that, we'll stop for dinner. We've definitely earned a nice meal out after all our hard work today."

Aunt Jayne grabbed her purse from the cupboard where they stored personal belongs. "Let's go then, shall we? Oh, I just realized, we should stop by and let Dexter out first."

"Yes," Uncle Oliver said. "Good idea. And Libby, I'm sorry you couldn't take him for a walk today. Tomorrow you can take him for a nice long one, how's that sound?"

She'd planned on going to Franny's house on Sunday to ask about the mysterious jar. That meant Dexter would have to come along.

Well, hopefully Franny liked dogs.

Chapter 10

Chocolate Fudge
comforting, like a happy memory

That night, with so much on her mind, Libby tossed and turned, unable to fall asleep. These were just a few of the questions that kept spinning around, making her brain feel like a merry-go-round:

Would Cedric be upset with her about not showing up at the grand opening? What should she tell him as to why she didn't make it?

Was her friendship with Rebecca over for good?

And finally, where was that jar with the poem? Now, more than ever, she wanted to read the poem about friendship and see if it offered some help or advice. Every time she considered that maybe she needed to let Rebecca go and move on, she'd remember a fun time they had together and long for more moments like that with her.

Like the time the two girls gathered up some friends and went Christmas caroling around the neighborhood. The pretty lights and the cool night air created the perfect atmosphere as the group sang their way from house to house. It had been a truly magical night. When they'd finished, Libby went to Rebecca's house for a sleepover. They slept on the floor, near the Christmas tree, where they'd exchanged whispers like gifts into the wee hours of the morning.

Didn't Rebecca remember any of the good times they'd had? Or did she just not care?

Libby rolled over again, and her charm bracelet poked her wrist. Thinking about Caitlin, Mia, and Hannah made her instantly feel better. She could picture the four of them, underneath the canopy of tree branches that smelled like pine, where they'd held friendship circle every afternoon.

Welcome to another meeting in the friendship circle. As it's been since the beginning, our friendship circle is secret, safe, and special. Speak your mind, but please be kind. And always

remember, no matter what, wherever we go, we're friends for-
ever, this we know.

Friends forever.

Forever.

Forever.

Finally, Libby drifted off to sleep.

The next day, Libby and Dexter headed out for their walk after lunch. They swung by the park on the way to Franny's house, because Libby thought maybe Cedric would be there. As much as she dreaded having to apologize about not coming to the grand opening, she wanted to get it over with. But he wasn't there. So they continued on to Franny's house, in her great-grandma's neighborhood.

As she walked past Grandma Grace's house, she wondered what would happen to it now. Would it be sold? She'd been ninety-three when she died, which meant there was probably a lot of stuff to go through before they could even put it up for sale.

When she reached Franny's house, the first thing Libby noticed was that it'd been painted recently. Instead of white, the house was now yellow. The second thing she noticed was the fancy new car in the driveway. Was someone visiting or was that car for Franny to drive?

She went to the front door and knocked. It didn't take long at all for someone to answer. "Good day," said the woman, who looked a little bit older than Aunt Jayne. "May I help you?"

"Hello. I'm here to see Franny?"

"I'm sorry, but Franny passed away. About a month ago. I'm her daughter, Anne. I'm actually here packing up her belongings so I can move in to the house next month. Is there something I can help you with?"

The news took Libby by surprise. She stood there for a moment, wondering what to do. "I'm very sorry for your loss. My great-grandmother Grace, who lived around the corner from here, passed away a couple of weeks ago. I came to ask Franny if she happened to have an old canning jar that Grace might have accidentally given to her. The jar came from America and was very special, so I'm trying to find it."

Anne shook her head. "I'm sorry, but it's not here."

Libby looked at her curiously. "But how do you know?"

Anne smiled. "My mother didn't keep anything like that. She hated clutter. She truly despised knickknacks and extra things that didn't serve a purpose. To give you an example, she only kept enough place settings for four people. She said she didn't need any more than that, because she'd never entertain more than one or two people at a time."

"So, you're sure?" Libby asked.

"Quite sure," Anne responded. "I'm sorry. I hope you find it. Do you have anywhere else you can look?"

"Yes. I have one more friend of hers to ask. Maybe I'll go there now."

"Tell you what," Anne said. "I'll go through the few kitchen items that are left to make sure it's not here. If I happen to find something, which I doubt, I'll let you know. Your family owns Mr. Pemberton's, right?"

"Yes."

"Good. I'll stop in there and leave a message for you if I find it. But as I said before, even if Grace did give it to Franny, I don't think Franny would have kept it." Anne laughed. "One year for Christmas I gave her a new set of glassware. Eight glasses in all. When I came by a week later, I looked in her cupboard and only saw four there. I checked the dishwasher, and they weren't there, so I asked her what she did with the other four. She told me she threw them out, because why did she need eight glasses if she only had four place settings? My mother was quite the character, let me tell you."

Tears started to form in Anne's eyes, and Libby knew that was her cue to leave.

"Thanks for your help," Libby said. "And again, I'm really sorry about your mother."

"I'm sorry for your loss as well," Anne said. "Good-bye."

Libby waved and scurried down the front walk. She knew she couldn't go home yet. She had to go to Eloise's house now, while she had the chance.

Her one and only last chance to find the jar.

Chapter 11

Lemon Drop
when life gives you lemons

Eloise lived just a few blocks over. Thankfully, it was a nice day, and pretty warm for early December, so the walk wasn't a big deal. Dexter certainly didn't mind continuing on. Libby was pretty sure he'd be happy to walk all day long, if given the chance.

Libby had been to Eloise's house only once, a couple of years ago, because Grandma Grace and Libby had made her a cake. A German chocolate cake, from scratch. Eloise had turned eighty years old, and Grandma Grace said turning eighty deserved something special. She'd said that Eloise didn't have any family nearby, and it made her sad to think she might not have cake for her special celebration.

It turned out that many of Eloise's friends had the same idea, so her kitchen was filled with delicious, homemade cakes. Anyone who stopped by could have any kind they wanted and as much as they wanted.

"Happy birthday to you," Libby had said to Eloise.

"And happy cake day to you," Eloise had said. "Come in and look at all my beautiful cakes, and see what you fancy."

Libby had decided on a piece of sour cherry crumb cake, and it was one of the best things she'd ever tasted. Of course, she'd had to try some of the German chocolate cake she and her great-grandma had made as well. It was good too, though a bit rich and filling when her stomach was already full of sour cherry crumb cake.

Cake day. That had been a wonderful day.

When Libby got to Eloise's house, she rubbed the charm bracelet for luck and knocked on the door three times.

But nobody answered. Libby tried again and still, nothing.

Just as she turned to leave, the gate along the side of the house clicked, and out walked Eloise wearing a straw hat on her head and carrying a couple of small garden tools.

"Hello," Libby said, walking toward her with Dexter by her side, wagging his tail.

"Why hello, dear," Eloise said. She was a very petite woman, only a little bit taller than Libby. She reached down and gave Dexter a few friendly pats. "I'm sorry, were you at the front door, looking for me?"

"Yes, I was. I don't know if you remember me. I'm Libby. Grace's great-granddaughter?"

Eloise smiled. "Why, yes. I remember now. She talked about you often. I do miss her so."

"Me too," Libby said.

"Let me put these tools away," Eloise said. "And then we'll go around back. It's a lovely fall day; we should make the most of it."

"All right," Libby said.

She waited as Eloise ducked into the garage for a moment. When the older woman returned, she led Libby through the gate and into her yard, which was a nice English garden with lots of trees, bushes, and colorful winter pansies.

"Wow," Libby said. "It's beautiful."

"Thank you."

"I guess I didn't see it the last time I was here because I was too busy eating cake."

Eloise chuckled. "Cake day was pretty exciting. I can see how you might have missed the garden."

They walked over to the patio, where there was a table and four chairs. "Have a seat, dear, and I'll get us some ice water. Unless you'd prefer some tea?"

"Water's fine," Libby said.

"The yard is completely fenced," Eloise said, "if you'd like to let your dog loose."

"Are you sure it's all right?"

She waved her hand as she approached the back door. "I'm sure. He's a little thing, he won't do any harm."

Libby let Dexter off his leash so he could have some fun exploring. A minute later, Eloise was back with two glasses of water, napkins, and a plate with some muffins. "It's not cake, but close," she said.

"Thank you."

"So, to what do I owe this pleasure, Libby?" she asked as she leaned back in her chair and took a long sip from her glass.

"I'm looking for something of Grandma Grace's, and I think you might have it."

"Me?" she asked with a look of surprise.

"There was a canning jar a friend of hers brought over

from America a long time ago. It was filled with peaches. After they ate the peaches, her friend wrote a poem about friendship, and Grandma Grace stuck it in the jar. But when she went looking for it recently, she couldn't find it. She thinks she may have put some flowers in it and given it to a friend. I'm trying to find it, because it was really special to her, and, well, I want to read the poem."

"She didn't give it to me," Eloise said as she picked up a muffin and took a bite.

"But I've checked with the other two friends she mentioned, and they don't have it either."

"Maybe it got thrown out," Eloise said. "Sad to consider, I know, but it very well could be that it's just . . . gone."

"I don't think so," Libby said, trying to convince herself as much as Eloise. "It was really special to her. Are you sure you don't have it? Maybe she gave it to you and you've forgotten?"

Eloise shook her head. "No. I'd remember something like that. The only time she gave me flowers was when I was ill, and they weren't in any kind of vase. Just wrapped together with a rubber band, and then we put them in one of my vases. I remember that quite clearly."

Libby wanted to ask her to check, just to be sure, but it didn't seem like Eloise had any doubt at all about the jar.

Eloise narrowed her eyes as if she were concentrating very hard. "You do know that even if the poem was in the jar, it most likely wouldn't be there now, right?"

Libby gave her a puzzled look. "What do you mean? Why not?"

"If Grace put flowers in the jar for a friend, either she would have put water in the jar before she delivered them, or the friend would have put some in once she received the flowers. Do you understand what I'm saying? The poem would have been ruined, if no one had noticed it was there."

Libby's mouth dropped open. Of course Eloise was right. Why hadn't Libby thought of that?

"Oh dear," Eloise said as tears filled Libby's eyes. "I've upset you. Here, have a lemon poppy seed muffin. They're quite good, if I do say so myself. It'll make you feel better."

Libby wasn't sure there was anything that would be able to do that.

Chapter 12

Banana Split Toffee
bursting with flavor

Monday morning, Libby went looking for Cedric before school. She had to make things right with him. She just had to. He was the only one who knew about her search for the jar and the poem, and she thought she might burst if she didn't tell someone how badly things had gone over the weekend.

She found him standing against the wall, waiting outside his first period class.

"Hi," she said.

"Hello."

"Did everything go all right on Saturday?" she asked.

"You would know the answer to that question if you'd come by like you said you would," he said as he picked at a bandage while holding his books against his chest.

"What happened to your finger?"

"I was helping my mother slice some cucumbers for a salad."

"Ouch," Libby said.

He continued to look at his finger, and Libby wondered if he was doing it on purpose, to avoid having to look at her. "Why do we have to eat salads anyway?" Cedric asked. "They taste like nothing. Like a whole lot of nothing with some goopy stuff poured on to try and make the nothing taste like something."

Libby smiled. "I'm sorry about your finger. And I'm sorry I didn't make it on Saturday. My aunt and uncle wouldn't let me go."

He stared at her quizzically. "What do you mean, your aunt and uncle? Were you visiting them?"

"That's who I live with," Libby explained. "My parents were killed in a car crash when I was little."

"That's horrible," Cedric said.

"It was," Libby said, leaning up against the wall next to Cedric. "But my aunt and uncle take good care of me. They're just a bit strict sometimes. Like, I can't have any electronics of my own until I turn thirteen."

"What, no phone?" Cedric asked.

Libby shook her head.

"No *computer*?" he said.

"Nope," Libby said.

"That's *really* horrible."

Libby laughed. "Anyway, was the grand opening a huge success? Did you have a lot of people?"

"I thought we did," Cedric said. "But my parents were disappointed. They think that other sweetshop in town with the old, stuffy name stole the customers away with their anniversary sale."

Libby gulped. Now was the time. She should tell him. Right now. She took a deep breath and tried to say the words, but nothing came out. How could she do it, she wondered. How could she tell him the truth and have him view her as one of the people responsible for possibly ruining his parents' dream? After all, if it hadn't been for the anniversary sale at Mr. Pemberton's, The Sweet Retreat probably would have had lots of business. In a way, his parents' disappointment about the grand opening was Libby's fault, since it'd been her idea to have an anniversary sale in the first place.

Shame filled her. She didn't want Cedric to know the truth, about any of it. She wanted things to stay exactly as they were.

Cedric turned and looked straight at her. "What's your favorite kind of candy?" he asked, changing the subject slightly. Libby felt relieved.

"Um, my favorite? Why do you want to know?"

"You told me Rebecca's favorite kind, but you've never told me yours. I think I've tasted just about everything in the shop now, and I'm really curious what your favorite is. I actually have a guess, and want to know if I'm right."

"What's your guess?"

"Gobstopper," Cedric said.

Libby shook her head. "Nope. Why do you think it's that one?"

Cedric shrugged. "I don't know. Maybe because it's kind of simple and old-fashioned? You seem like a simple girl who likes simple things."

"Wait," Libby said, crossing her arms. "I'm not sure I like the sound of that. What do you mean, *simple*?"

"I don't mean anything bad by it. Honest. It just seems to me that you're not someone who needs or wants fancy things. Take that jar you've been looking for. Nothing fancy about it, right?"

Libby's face drooped. "Right. The jar. I have bad news about that."

"You do?" A boy walked by and slapped Cedric on the shoulder. Cedric glanced up, waved, and then looked back at Libby. "What happened?"

Traffic was picking up in the hallway. Libby glanced at her watch and saw that she only had a minute before the bell would ring. She spoke quickly. "One of the ladies, Franny, died, and her daughter was sure it wasn't in her house. The other lady, Eloise, said she doesn't have it either. But what's even worse is Eloise told me if Grandma Grace did give it away to someone with flowers, the poem wouldn't still be there, because the water put in the vase to keep the flowers fresh would have destroyed it."

"Maybe your grandma noticed the piece of paper and took it out before she gave the jar away," Cedric suggested.

"But if she noticed the poem," Libby argued, "she would have realized it was the special jar and not given it away at all. Do you see what I mean?"

"Except it doesn't seem like she gave it away if her three friends don't have it," Cedric said.

Libby shook her head, confused.

"Where are you going to look next?" Cedric asked.

Libby sighed. "I think I need to see if I can get into Grandma Grace's house and search for it there. Maybe she just didn't look hard enough."

The bell rang and the door to Cedric's first period class opened.

"I should get to class," Libby said.

"Do you want to meet at the park later?" Cedric asked. "After school? I need to walk Goldie, since she didn't get out much this weekend."

"Sure," Libby said. She waved and turned to leave. "See you then."

"Wait. You didn't tell me what your favorite kind of candy is."

Libby smiled. "Keep guessing. It will be fun to see how long it takes you to figure it out."

Libby told herself that when Cedric figured it out, when he guessed correctly, *that* would be when she'd tell him. About Mr. Pemberton's. It would be the perfect opportunity.

A small voice inside of her whispered that she shouldn't wait. That it might take Cedric a really long time to guess, and it wasn't right to keep the truth from him. But Libby shook her head, trying to shake that voice away.

More time was exactly what she needed, for it would give The Sweet Retreat a chance to take off and do well. Once that happened, it would be much easier to tell Cedric about her family's business. After all, she couldn't bear to have him think of her, specifically, as the enemy.

It made her shudder just thinking about it.

Chapter 13

Sweet Banana Candy
big and yellow, can't miss it

When Libby got home from school, she grabbed Dexter's leash, told her aunt where she was headed, and took off. She didn't even take the time to have a snack. It seemed Cedric had forgiven her for not making it to the grand opening on Saturday, and she didn't want to do anything else that might upset him.

She and Dexter walked around the park, looking for Cedric, but he wasn't there yet. As she walked by a girl sitting at a picnic table, the girl looked up from whatever it was she was working on and said, "Hello. Don't you go to my school?"

Libby didn't recognize the girl. "I don't know. I go to Bennett Memorial."

"Yes," the girl said. "We're in choir together."

Libby felt bad for not recognizing her, even though it was a big class. She was about to apologize for it when the girl asked, "Do you want to sit with me for a few minutes?"

Libby shrugged. "All right. Just until my friend gets here."

After Libby sat down, the girl said, "I'm Sabrina, by the way."

"I'm Libby. And this is Dexter."

"He's cute," Sabrina said with a smile. "I was drawing him. See?"

Libby leaned in to take a look at the tablet of paper on the table. She had indeed sketched a picture of Dexter. "Wow. You're a really good artist."

"Thanks," Sabrina said. "I have another pencil, if you'd like to draw too."

"Sure." Libby put Dexter's leash on the ground and stepped on it, so she'd have both hands free. Dexter settled down in a spot on the grass and seemed perfectly content.

Sabrina reached into her bag and got out a drawing pencil and another sketch pad. "I always bring two, just in case I run into a friend."

Libby began to draw the trunk of a tree as she looked out at one in the park. "My friend Cedric, who I'm supposed to meet here, loves to draw too. He makes his own comic books."

"Nifty," Sabrina said.

Libby looked up. "Did you just say *nifty*?"

"Yes," Sabrina said. "I love that word. How come we don't say it much anymore? Everyone says *brilliant* or *splendid*, but I like *nifty*."

Libby watched Sabrina as she continued to work on her picture of Dexter. Sabrina had short brown hair and pretty brown eyes. She wore green overalls with a pink tee underneath. She looked a bit old-fashioned and trendy all at the same time. In fact, she looked exactly like someone who would love the word *nifty*.

"So, you like to draw too?" Sabrina asked.

"Yes," Libby said.

"My mum thinks I'm strange because I always have my nose in a book or a pencil in my hand. She tells me, 'Go outside. You need fresh air. Children need fresh air.'"

"So you come here and draw?" Libby asked. "That's pretty smart."

"As long as the weather's nice. It's not as fun when it's pouring."

"What kind of books do you like to read?" Libby asked.

Sabrina looked up from her drawing, her eyes big and round. "Mysteries. I can't get enough of them. I love trying to figure it all out. Put the pieces of the puzzle together or whatever."

"I have a real-life mystery that I'm trying to solve right now," Libby said. "I think it must be much more fun to read about a mystery rather than try to solve one yourself."

Sabrina put her pencil down. "Oh, you have to tell me. Maybe I can help you solve it. Please?"

Libby put the final touches on her tree and then set her pencil down too. She looked around, wondering if she'd missed Cedric while she was busy drawing. But she didn't see him or Goldie anywhere. "All right. I'll tell you."

And so, she told Sabrina the entire story of the jar and the poem. How she'd learned about it by reading her great grandmother's journal, and then how she went looking for it at the three places Grandma Grace thought it might be.

"I bet it's in her house," Sabrina said after Libby had

finished her story. "When she moved, it got put in a strange place, and it's just a matter of finding it."

"That's exactly what I've been thinking," Libby said, resting her chin in her hands. "I guess I have to figure out how to get into her house. Like, should I ask my aunt and uncle if they can take me there, or do I try to sneak in?"

"No one is living there now?" Sabrina said.

"Nope."

"Are they going to sell the house?"

"I don't know," Libby said. "I haven't heard them say anything."

"I think you should try to sneak in. That way you can look anywhere and everywhere without worrying about it. All you need is a window you can open that you can crawl through, right?"

"What if someone sees me?" Libby asked, trying to imagine crawling through a window. "Or even worse, what if I get stuck?"

"I could go with you," Sabrina said.

Libby took a deep breath. "I need to think about it. I'll let you know at school in a couple of days, how's that?"

Sabrina nodded. "All right. I understand." She looked at her watch. "I have to get home."

Libby handed the art supplies back to her. "Thanks for letting me draw with you."

"You're welcome. Do you think your friend is coming?"

Libby looked around the park again. The sun was setting low in the sky and it was getting chilly. "I don't think so. Guess I'll head home too."

"I'm glad he didn't show up," Sabrina said. "I loved hearing about your mystery."

Libby wasn't sure what Cedric's absence meant, exactly, but of all the things she felt about it, glad wasn't one of them. It was nice getting to know Sabrina, of course. But she worried all over again that he was upset about her not showing up on Saturday.

Maybe this had been payback?

Chapter 14

Pink Sugar Mouse
tastes better than you'd expect

Libby found Cedric at school the next day.

"You didn't come," Libby said as she watched him fight with a pile of books in his locker. "To the park. I waited for you for quite a while."

Cedric turned around and faced her. "Oh, you actually went? I didn't think you'd show up, so I didn't go."

Libby crossed her arms and scowled. She'd been right. He'd wanted to pay her back for not showing up at the grand opening. "That's not very nice, Cedric. I already told you I'm sorry I couldn't make it on Saturday. Why did you have to make me feel even worse?"

He looked down at his feet and didn't say anything for a few seconds. Finally he looked at her. "I'm sorry. You're right.

It wasn't very nice. I got home and I was tired and all I wanted to do was sit and draw, so that's what I did."

"If you'd come to the park, you could have sketched with me and Sabrina."

He gave her a puzzled look. "Who's Sabrina?"

"I met her yesterday. She goes here too. She's a really good artist."

"Well fine," he said as he went back to his locker. "See? You didn't need me there anyway."

There was something in his voice that made Libby feel bad about being so annoyed with him. He sounded down. Sad, maybe. "Is something wrong, Cedric?" Libby asked. "You're acting a bit strange, and I think I'm worried about you."

"Nah, don't worry about me." After he had his books, he shut his locker door and turned to face her. "We may be living on the streets soon, eating the sweets we couldn't sell, but we'll be fine."

Libby felt a little knife stab at her heart. "Cedric, what's going on? Tell me. Please?"

The bell rang. He shook his head. "I have to get to class. See you later."

She didn't want him to go to class. He should stay so they could work things out. Whatever was going on, she wanted to try and help him. But of course he didn't stay. School was about to start. And so, Libby went to class like she was supposed to and hoped that soon, they would get the chance to talk some more.

In choir class later, Sabrina was waiting for Libby.

"Hi," she said, patting the chair next to her. "I saved you a seat."

The class spent the first fifteen minutes warming up their voices before they took their places on the risers. They could sit anywhere they wanted during those fifteen minutes.

"Thanks," Libby said.

"Any more news about the jar since yesterday?" Sabrina asked.

Libby sighed. "I read through Grandma Grace's journal again before bed, wondering if I missed something about the jar and the poem. But I didn't find anything. I think at dinner tonight, I'll ask my aunt and uncle if they'll take me to her house. I don't want to sneak in and get in trouble."

"I understand," Sabrina said. "It would have been fun to snoop through the house with you, though. Remember, you must think like a detective."

Libby furrowed her brow. "How do I do that?"

"You have to put yourself in your great-grandma's shoes. What I mean by that is, think like her, not like you."

"That's not going to be very easy," Libby said.

"Detective work is definitely not easy," Sabrina said. "Rewarding? Yes. But easy? No way."

"Great," Libby muttered as the bell rang, letting them know class was about to start.

When Libby got home from school, there was a letter waiting for her, from Caitlin. She sat at the table and read it while having some biscuits and tea.

Dear Libby,

How are you? How's the charm bracelet? Is it bringing you lots of luck? I hope so. You deserve it. I can't wait to see what new charms are added when it's my turn again.

Things have been going really well here. Our play, <u>Charlotte's Web</u>, is happening next weekend. I've had a blast being in the cast (hey, that rhymes) with my friends Esther and Tezra. We've already decided we're going to try out for the spring play too. Not sure what it's going to be yet, but it doesn't matter. We'll have fun whatever it is. We're also on a Battle of the Books team together, and we just got the book list with sixteen wonderful books we have to read. We're going to divide the list up so we don't have to read all of the books, but between you and me, I might try to read all of them anyway. When we have the battles, and have to answer questions about the books, I want to be able to help my friends if they need it, you know?

How's it going at the new school? Hopefully by now you've made some new friends too. I know it can be hard. I really do. But, Libby you have to know anyone would feel so lucky to call you friend. I sure do!

Time to go help my mom make dinner. Please write

to me and tell me how you are and what's going on. I miss you like crazy!

Your cabin 7 BFF,
Caitlin

She folded the letter and put it away. It made Libby happy to know that Caitlin was having fun with her new friends. But she couldn't deny that she felt envious about it all too. She wanted friends like that. More than anything, that's what she wanted.

Rebecca used to be that kind of friend. No matter what they did together, they had a good time. Now when she thought of Rebecca, she thought of the awkwardness that had developed between them and the way she looked at Libby like she almost couldn't stand her.

Libby had been so excited to be reunited with her bestie when she'd returned from camp in August. But Rebecca hadn't returned her calls for days. When they'd finally met up at their favorite café for some tea and cake, it seemed like every other word out of Rebecca's mouth was a person's name Libby had never heard before. She'd met a new group of kids while Libby had been gone over the summer, and while Libby understood the excitement, since she'd made new friends too, what she couldn't understand was how Rebecca didn't seem to want to talk about *anything* else.

It got really annoying when Rebecca had gone on and on about this one boy, Seth, and his adorable dimples and beautiful blue eyes. When Libby'd tried to tell her about camp, Rebecca had shut her down fast, making some rude comment about how boring it must have been without any boys to flirt with. Libby had argued with her about how it hadn't been boring at all, that she'd actually *liked* the fact that there weren't any boys to worry about.

Libby had gone home feeling as if a stranger had taken over Rebecca's body. It felt like she hardly knew her anymore. Hoping it'd just been a weird, one-time thing, Libby had attempted a couple of other get-togethers, and both times were complete disasters. Rebecca had gotten bored in a matter of minutes and spent the rest of the time texting her new friends on her fancy smartphone and showing Libby photos of all of them.

Soon after school started, they'd run into each other once at the park, and what used to be a fun and comfortable friendship now felt strange and uneasy.

Was it possible to change that? Did she even want to any more?

Of course I do, she thought.

Just then, the telephone rang. Her aunt called from the other room, where she was sewing, "Can you get that, Libby?"

Libby picked up the phone. "Hello?"

"Hello, may I speak to Libby, please?" It was the voice of an older woman, but Libby couldn't quite place who it was.

"This is she."

"Libby, this is Margaret, Grandma Grace's friend. I have some news for you. I think I may have found the jar you've been looking for. I'm sorry that we missed it when you were here before."

Libby's heartbeat quickened. "You really think you've found it? Wow. That's . . . amazing."

"I believe so," she said. "But I think you're going to be quite surprised, because it's not exactly what you expected to find. Are you able to come over on Saturday and see it for yourself?"

"Yes," Libby said. "Yes, I can do that."

"All right, good. I'll see you then."

"Thanks for letting me know. Good-bye."

"Good-bye."

Libby hung up the phone feeling happy, but also confused. What had she meant when she'd said, "it's not exactly what you expected?"

Whatever it was, Libby couldn't wait to find out. If only Saturday wasn't four long days away.

Chapter 15

Butter Mint
picture perfect

"I have some news," Libby's uncle said that night as the family finished up their dinner.

"I hope it's good news," Aunt Jayne said.

"Do either of you know what today is?" Uncle Oliver asked after he finished wiping his mouth with his napkin and put it on his empty plate.

Aunt Jayne and Libby looked at each other. "Tuesday?" Libby replied.

"Well, yes," Uncle Oliver said. "That's true. But it's also December third, and you know what that means?"

Libby felt silly that she had no clue what that meant. Had she forgotten someone's birthday?

"Oliver," Aunt Jayne said, "I don't know what you're talking about. Can you please just tell us?"

He laughed. "All right, all right, I'll tell you. I thought you might remember, but I guess not. December third is the day we officially declare it the holiday season at Mr. Pemberton's Olde Sweetshop. It's been that way for as long as I can remember, and I've upheld that tradition since I've been in charge."

Libby's face lit up. "Did you get out the boxes of holiday decorations today?"

"I sure did," Uncle Oliver said. "I have a few things I need help with, so I thought we'd all go over and finish up there in a bit."

"Are you going to decorate the front door like a big wrapped gift again?" Libby asked.

"Yes, just like every year." He scooted his chair back from the table. "But that's not actually my news. My news is that because the holiday season is officially upon us, I've decided to run an ad in the newspaper over the next few weeks. And here's the exciting part — you two are going to be a part of it!"

Libby narrowed her eyes. "What do you mean?"

"We're going to have our picture taken," her uncle explained with a smile. "In front of our wonderful sweetshop. I want people to know our faces and be comfortable shopping with us. I'm thinking of it as an invitation, of sorts." He cleared his throat and in a cheerful voice said, "Come one, come all, and join us this holiday season!"

Libby did not like this idea. She didn't want the world to know her family owned the sweetshop. Kids at school might treat her differently. They might assume if she became their friend, they could have all the candy they wanted. And of course, she *really* didn't want Cedric to know her family owned the shop. Not yet, anyway. It had to be the perfect time to tell him. And she'd already decided that when he guessed her favorite candy, *that* would be the perfect time to tell him.

"I think just the two of you should be in the photo," Libby said. "Without me."

"That's no fun," her aunt said as she stood up and started clearing away the dishes. "It's a family business, and you are a part of it. It wouldn't be right if you weren't in it."

"But, do you think it's safe?" Libby asked, standing up to help with the dishes.

"Yes, of course it's safe," Uncle Oliver said. "We won't give out your name. And it won't be too close up, because we want to get the entire storefront into the shot."

This actually made Libby feel better. "It won't be completely obvious that it's me, then?" she asked.

"Right," Uncle Oliver said. "But we'll know it's you, and our faithful customers will know it's you, and it will remind them of our little store and how wonderful it is to shop there during the holidays. And for people not familiar with us, our smiling faces will encourage them to come and get to know us."

Libby considered all of this carefully, along with the fact that most kids didn't sit down and read the newspaper like adults did. Chances were, Cedric wouldn't see the ad, and if he did happen to see it, hopefully he wouldn't recognize Libby.

"All right," Libby said. "If this is really what you want, I'll go along with it."

"Wonderful," Uncle Oliver said. "Thank you, love. And to show my appreciation, I'll give you the weekend off from filling the jars. Getting your photo taken will be all the work you have to do. How's that?"

"Wonderful," Libby said, trying to sound excited. She was pretty sure she'd done a lousy job, though.

The next day before school, Libby was at her locker when she heard Cedric behind her say, "I wore my lucky trousers today."

Libby turned around and looked at them. Then her eyes met his. "How come?"

"I feel bad. About not showing up at the park. So I wore them because I hope that we can forget all of that and go back to walking our dogs together like nothing happened."

"Great," Libby said.

"Great?"

"Yes. Things were feeling strange between us, and I didn't like it."

"Me neither," Cedric said as Libby closed the locker door, her books in hand. "I have lots of homework, but I should be able to go to the park on Saturday. What about you?"

Libby bit her lip. She couldn't tell him about the photo shoot. "I, uh, have to go see Margaret about the jar."

"Do I know who Margaret is?" Cedric asked as they began walking.

"She's the first friend of Grandma Grace's that I went and visited. She rang yesterday and said she thinks she's found the jar. She asked me to come and see her on Saturday, so she could show me."

"That's exciting," Cedric said. "But it won't take all day. Let's plan on meeting up after that. How about at four?"

Uncle Oliver hadn't told her what time the photo shoot was scheduled for. Hopefully it would be earlier in the day. "All right. But what if it takes longer than I expect?"

"I'm going to give you my cell phone number so you can ring me," Cedric said, pulling his phone out of his pocket.

"I don't have a phone though," Libby said. "Remember? Not until I'm thirteen."

"Well, write down my number anyway, and you can use Margaret's phone if you have to."

Libby pulled a piece of paper out of her bag and handed it to Cedric. "Here, you can write it down."

When that was done, Cedric gave the paper back to her and said, "I still want to know your favorite candy."

"And I want you to guess," Libby replied.

"Can I have a hint? Like, is it chocolate or not?"

"Not."

"Is it something strange, like Dracula teeth?" he asked.

"Ew, no," Libby said, stopping outside the door of her classroom. "But remember, what's strange to one person isn't to another. You know, like Rebecca's favorite, chocolate frogs. I think they're totally strange, but she loves them more than anything."

"Sweet bananas?" he asked.

"Nope."

"Licorice toffee?"

She shook her head and the bell rang. "Looks like your lucky trousers aren't working very well today. Sorry."

"I'm going to figure it out," Cedric said.

"It's probably going to take you a while," Libby said before she turned around and left.

Hopefully, a long while, she thought to herself.

Chapter 16

Laffy Taffy
hard not to giggle

Saturday morning, Libby woke up and got herself ready. The photo shoot was scheduled for one o'clock, so she'd decided the day before that she would go and see Margaret in the morning. Margaret hadn't given a specific time to stop by, so Libby figured any time was probably fine.

While she ate her porridge, she told her aunt that she was going to go and visit Margaret again.

"Are you sure it's all right?" Aunt Jayne asked. "I mean, you aren't making a pest out of yourself, are you?"

"No," Libby said. "She asked me to stop by and see her again. She likes having me over, I promise."

"Hm. I suppose she does, then. But don't stay too long.

We have to decide what to wear for the photo shoot. We don't want our outfits to clash, you know."

"Right," Libby agreed. "But we also don't want to be matchy-matchy. That would look ridiculous."

"Yes," her aunt said. "We want to complement each other." She chuckled. "I suppose we could have used this photo shoot as an excuse to go shopping. I didn't even think of that."

One thing about Aunt Jayne: she loved shopping, especially for clothes.

"You know, we have a few hours," Aunt Jayne said as she eyed the clock. "We could go shopping now. You could visit Margaret another day."

Libby groaned as she got up and took her bowl to the sink. "But I don't want to go shopping. It's bad enough I have to spend part of my Saturday getting my picture taken. Last Saturday I worked at the shop all day. Can't I please have this morning to do what I want to do?"

Aunt Jayne rubbed Libby's back and said, "Yes. You can. I'm sorry, I didn't know shopping for new clothes was such a chore. Most girls your age love to shop."

"Yes, but that's when they're shopping because they

want to, not because they have to buy something for a silly advertisement."

Her aunt clucked her tongue. "Now, now, it's not silly. It's actually very smart, what your uncle is doing. The month of December is our biggest month of the year, we have to do what we can to make it as successful as possible."

"I know. I'm sorry. I didn't mean anything bad by it."

"It's all right. You go along and see Margaret and have a lovely time. Be back here by eleven-thirty, please."

"I will," Libby said. "See you then."

It was a chilly December day, and the gray, cloudy sky looked like it might open up and pour any second. Libby decided she better grab an umbrella, just in case. She ran back inside and got one from the hall closet and then went on her way to Margaret's cottage.

As she walked, she decided she needed to remember something from camp to keep her mind occupied. She was so curious about what Margaret had waiting for her, she could hardly stand it.

Libby took the bracelet off of one wrist and clasped it onto the other.

She smiled as she remembered the night they snuck out of Cabin 7 so they could play a joke on the Cabin 2 girls.

Cabin 2 seemed to be filled with girls who thought they were better than everyone else. If there was a way for them to set themselves apart from the crowd, they found it. It seemed like they wanted to be noticed. All the time.

They developed a special language that only the girls in Cabin 2 knew. And one girl in Cabin 2 had brought along special pink bandanas for her cabin mates. Each of the girls wore a bandana proudly, either around the neck or on the head or like an armband.

During the second week of camp, someone had gone around to each cabin during the night and put plastic wrap across every doorway. Girls opened the doors and walked right into the stuff, squealing as they did because it surprised them so much.

Although every cabin had been included in the prank, when the girls in Cabin 2 came out for the first time that morning, someone saw the plastic wrap and took it down. It was so totally obvious to the girls in the other cabins that the Cabin 2 girls knew to look for the plastic wrap.

There was lots of finger pointing, but no one ever came forward and admitted to the prank. Still, the girls in Cabin 7 had decided to get back at the girls in Cabin 2. So, one night they snuck out and covered the porch of Cabin 2 with lots of shaving cream and hair conditioner. The hope was that when the Cabin 2 girls walked out the next morning, they would slip and slide like they were trying to walk across an ice rink.

Libby could remember trying not to laugh as she worked alongside Mia, Caitlin, and Hannah. They'd promised each other, over and over again, that they would stay as quiet as possible. It was just so funny, sneaking out in the dark, and covering the porch with slimy stuff.

When Libby arrived at Margaret's cottage, she had a smile on her face. She didn't know what she'd find waiting for her when she went through that purple door, but one thing she knew for sure — whatever it was, she could be glad that she wouldn't run into plastic wrap or slip and slide across shaving cream.

Chapter 17

Jelly Bean
your tongue might change color

"Good morning, Libby," Margaret said when she opened the door. She glanced up at the sky and added, "Looks like a storm is brewing, doesn't it? Please, come in."

"I brought my umbrella," Libby said. "Just in case."

"Here, let me take your jacket for you," Margaret said as she reached up to help Libby take it off. She hung it in the hall closet along with the umbrella.

"Come into the kitchen," Margaret said, "and I'll show you what I found."

"I can't wait to see," Libby said, rubbing her hands together.

Margaret walked over to the kitchen table and Libby followed her. There, in the middle of the table, was a light purple jar.

Libby gave Margaret a curious look. "I don't understand. She specifically said it was a clear canning jar."

"Yes, I know," Margaret replied. "Please, take a seat. I have a story to tell you that I think you'll find quite interesting."

Libby did as she was told, staring at the purple jar the whole time.

Margaret sat across from her. "A friend came to visit me a few days ago, and she drank out of the 'good luck' teacup you had last time. I mentioned your visit and how you were looking for a special jar your great-grandmother had that came from America. My friend Bee asked me if I might have a colored canning jar in my cupboard. I told her I didn't know, because we hadn't been looking for a colored jar, we'd been looking for a clear jar.

"She asked if she could look through my collection, and so I agreed. When she pulled out this jar, she said, 'I think this is what the girl might have been looking for.'"

"But why?" Libby asked. "Why would she think that?"

Margaret laughed. "That's what I asked her. You see, Bee knows her antiques very well. And she knows that during the First World War, a certain ingredient they used in canning jars was cut off by German blockades." She stood up and went to the counter, where she picked up her reading glasses and a piece of paper. "I wrote it down because I knew I wouldn't remember the name." She read the words off the piece of paper. "Manganese dioxide. Bee said prior to the start of World War One, manufacturers used manganese dioxide as their chemical agent of choice to clarify glass. But when manufacturers couldn't get it because of the war, they switched to a different chemical, selenium, instead. And they didn't change back later."

Libby shook her head. "I'm so confused."

Margaret sat down again. "I know. It *is* confusing. You see, Libby, we now know that when a jar with manganese dioxide is exposed to sunlight, the glass reacts to the sunlight and it changes color."

"Changes color?" Libby asked. She looked at the purple jar and then back at Margaret. "You mean, it changes from clear to light purple?"

"Yes. That's exactly what I mean. We didn't notice this jar when you were here before because it wasn't clear. Your grandma must not have realized this was her special jar, because it was a different color than she remembered."

"Wow," Libby said, looking at the jar differently now. "So whenever you find a purple canning jar that looks like this one, you know it was made before the First World War?"

"Yes," Margaret said. "They are not easy to find. Many people collect them, for as time goes on, they'll be more and more valuable."

"But Mae visited Grandma Grace in the forties," Libby said. "That was a long time after World War One."

"Maybe the jar had belonged to her mother," Margaret replied. "Or someone else in her family. It's hard to know, really."

One question still lingered in Libby's mind. She knew the chances were slim to none, but still, she had to ask. "What about the poem? Did you find any sign of it?"

Margaret set her reading glasses on the table. "I'm afraid not, no. It's hard to know what may have happened to it. She may not have even noticed it was in the jar when she gave it to me, in which case, the poem wouldn't have survived the water and the flowers."

Libby stared at the table, trying not to show her disappointment.

"May I ask why you are so interested in that poem?" Margaret asked.

"It probably sounds silly," Libby said, "but I hoped it would help me with the problems I'm having with my best friend. When I read about the jar and Mae's poem in Grandma Grace's journal, it felt like it was a sign. A sign that I should find it and maybe it would tell me what to do about Rebecca."

Margaret nodded sympathetically. "You know, poems are often about feelings. Mae probably wrote it to tell your great-grandma how much her friendship meant to her."

Libby thought about this for a second. "So, it wouldn't have really given me any advice?"

"My guess to that question is no, probably not. I'm sure it would have been fun to read, but it probably wouldn't have been very helpful to you."

Libby sat up straight as an idea came to her out of the blue. "Maybe I don't need to read the poem after all," she said. "Maybe I just need to know that when Mae wanted to tell her friend how much she meant to her, she used poetry to do that. And if I'm looking for a way to tell Rebecca how much she means to me and how much I miss her, maybe I should try writing a poem too."

Margaret raised her eyebrows. "I think you're onto something, Libby."

Libby sunk back into her seat again. "But I don't know how to write poetry. I know they don't all have to rhyme, but still, it seems like it would be hard. I don't think we study poetry in school until next year."

"Do you know what a haiku is?" Margaret asked.

"I'm not sure," Libby said. "I think I've heard of it, but . . ."

"It's a very popular type of poetry," Margaret explained. "When I was a teacher years ago, I'd have my students create haiku. We'd go outside and the kids would take notes about the things we saw, paying special attention to the weather, the sky, and the trees and plants. Then they'd come back inside and put their thoughts and feelings into the five, seven, five format. That is, the first line has five syllables, the second line has seven syllables, and the third line has five again. They really enjoyed it. Let me see if I can do one for you as an example."

Margaret went to the counter again and got a pen and a piece of paper. She worked for a few minutes on her poem and then she read it out loud to Libby.

"Warm tea and biscuits
soothe the heart and frazzled nerves,
like a faithful friend."

"I love that," Libby said. "I'll have to try it."

"Here," Margaret said, "you can have this one as an example. Remember, five, seven, five. And it's perfectly fine to count out the rhythm using your fingers." She chuckled. "I do it all the time."

Libby took the poem and then she stood up. "Thanks for your help. I should get home. We're doing a photo shoot for Mr. Pemberton's pretty soon, and I need to get ready."

Margaret picked up the jar and handed it to Libby. "Don't forget this."

Libby's eyes got wide. "But it's yours."

"No. I want you to have it. Maybe you won't ever find the poem from Mae to Grace, but this jar can be a reminder to you that friends are kind and generous with each other. Mae brought peaches all the way over from America in this jar, as a token of her friendship. And then, many years later, your great-grandma gave it to me with some flowers, another lovely gesture. Friendship is about giving and receiving. Not just of things, but of time and thoughts and feelings. Let this jar remind you of that, sweet Libby. All right?"

Libby took the jar and hugged it close to her chest. Something told her that the time she'd just spent with Margaret, listening to her wise words, was probably more helpful than any poem might have been.

Chapter 18

Licorice Twists
perfect for a rainy day

All the way home, Libby couldn't stop thinking about what Margaret had said.

Friendship is about giving and receiving.

It was like the friendship bracelet she shared with her camp friends. They took turns wearing it, adding a new charm each time — giving and receiving the bracelet over and over again. Now, more than ever, it seemed like the perfect symbol of their friendship.

But what about Rebecca? She and Libby didn't have anything like that. Would they ever get back to a place where they happily shared each other's time and thoughts and feelings, like Margaret had said?

Libby just knew she should write Rebecca a poem and try to express how she felt about all of this. The thought of doing that in three little lines seemed nearly impossible, however. Margaret made it look so easy, the same way Cedric made drawing comic books look easy.

Libby was so glad Cedric had shared that part of himself with Libby, a part he probably didn't share with many people. It showed he felt comfortable with her and trusted her to not laugh or make fun of him, but to accept him for the person he was.

And she did. So why was she so scared about him accepting her the same way? Mostly, about accepting that her family owned the other sweetshop in town? Why didn't she give Cedric more credit than that? He was a nice guy, who liked dogs and going for walks and making art. He'd understand, wouldn't he?

By the time Libby got home, she felt really horrible about keeping this big part of her life a secret from him. If she wanted to stay friends with Cedric, and she did, she realized she needed to tell him the truth. Today. She couldn't wait any longer, because it just wasn't right.

When she walked in the front door, she heard her aunt and uncle talking in the kitchen.

"I'm home," Libby called as she took off her coat and hung it in the coat closet.

"Oh good," Aunt Jayne replied. "We could use your opinion, Libby. Come and tell us what you think."

She went into the kitchen and found the two of them looking at a couple of ties Jayne held up in each of her hands. One was red with green-and-white stripes while the other one was paisley done in light green and blue colors.

"Which one do you like better?" Aunt Jayne asked.

"The one that doesn't scream Christmas," Libby said as she set the canning jar down on the counter before she went to get a drink of water.

"See?" Jayne said to Oliver. "Just like I thought. The shop's lovely decorations will say happy holidays, so your tie doesn't have to."

Uncle Oliver chuckled. "All right. You win."

"Who's covering the shop while you pick out a tie to wear?" Libby asked.

"Papa and Nana," Uncle Oliver said. "They're staying at Grandma Grace's house for the rest of the month. You know how much they enjoy helping out around the holidays."

Her grandpa Pemberton (whom she called Papa) and Uncle Oliver had worked at the sweetshop together for years before Papa finally decided to retire. Papa and Nana lived in London now, so they didn't help out much around the shop anymore, except during December.

Uncle Oliver picked up the purple jar. "What's this?"

Libby set down her water glass as she said, "A gift from Margaret. It belonged to Grandma Grace."

He turned it over in his hands. "Wow. Is it old?"

"Yes," Libby said. "A friend brought it over from America on a ship. We're pretty sure, because of the color, it was made before the First World War."

"That was very nice of Margaret to give it to you," Aunt Jayne said. "In the spring, it will make a lovely vase."

"Can I keep it in my room?" Libby asked.

"Sure," Aunt Jayne replied. Oliver handed Libby the jar, and then Jayne handed Oliver the ties.

"Shall I go get dressed, then?" Uncle Oliver asked.

"Let's have a bite to eat first, and then we'll all change," Aunt Jayne said, turning toward the refrigerator.

"Ah, brilliant idea," Uncle Oliver said. "That way we don't risk spilling anything on our nice clothes." He snuggled up to his wife and gave her a kiss on the cheek. "Since I let you pick out my tie, do I get to pick out what dress you wear?"

"No," both Jayne and Libby said, quite loudly. Everyone laughed.

Uncle Oliver threw his hands in the air. "My taste isn't that awful, is it?"

Libby looked at her aunt. Then Aunt Jayne nicely said, "Oliver, that green-and-red tie is hideous. I can't even imagine why you bought it in the first place. And then to think it would be a good idea to wear it today?"

"But it's festive," he argued. "Don't you like festive?"

"Except we really don't need to be walking Christmas trees," Aunt Jayne said. "No, Libby and I can manage just fine choosing what we wear this afternoon."

In the end, Libby chose a simple black skirt and an off-white sweater with a pretty lace collar. Her aunt Jayne wore a light green dress that matched Uncle Oliver's tie almost perfectly.

As they started to step outside, they stopped. It was raining.

Jayne looked at Oliver. "Do you think we should reschedule? I'm not sure the drowned-rat look will sell sweets very well."

"There's no time for that," Uncle Oliver said. "We need the photo done today so we can run the ad next week. Remember, the shop has a nice-sized awning. We'll stand under that and we should stay dry. For the most part."

But as they drove to the shop, the rain came down harder and harder. When they arrived, the three of them ran inside the shop and found the photographer, Mr. Liken, waiting for them, along with his assistant.

"I think it would be best to do the photo shoot another day," Mr. Liken said.

Uncle Oliver explained the urgency of the situation and pleaded with him to take a few photos for them. "We can be quick about it. And we don't need anything too elaborate."

As Oliver and Mr. Liken talked the situation over, Libby went to speak to Papa and Nana. After they greeted her with a hug, her nana asked, "How are you? Anything exciting happening in Libby's world?"

Libby quickly told them about the purple jar, because she figured her nana would like to hear the story, since Grandma Grace had been her mother.

"Mother talked a lot about Mae," Nana said. "They were good friends for a long, long time."

"I guess Mae wrote a sweet poem when she came to visit all those years ago," Libby said. "Grandma Grace said she'd stuck it in the jar, but it's not there anymore. I wish I could have read it."

"All right, Libby," Uncle Oliver called out just then. "Time to step outside and smile like we are absolutely thrilled to be standing in the middle of a big rainstorm. Don't worry, we'll try to get this over with in a hurry."

"See you later," Libby said to her grandparents.

Papa and Nana gave her a little wave as Libby hurried over to her aunt and uncle. Mr. Liken's assistant held a very large umbrella for Mr. Liken to stand under while Oliver, Jayne, and Libby huddled up against the building, underneath the awning. The three of them tried their best to look like they were happy about the whole rain-drenched situation.

As they posed and smiled, changing their posture or

positioning according to Mr. Liken's instructions, Libby realized something.

If the nasty weather continued, the dog walk later would be impossible. And if she couldn't walk the dog and meet up with Cedric, she couldn't tell him what she really, really needed to tell him.

It had to stop raining. It just had to.

Chapter 19

Candy Stick
difficult to share

After the photo shoot, Libby rode home with her aunt while her uncle stayed at the shop so his parents wouldn't have to worry about closing up later in the day.

Libby kept eyeing the clock, wondering if the weather would let up in time to meet Cedric at the park. She and her aunt got home around three that afternoon, each going their separate ways to change out of their nice clothes.

Once she was comfortable in jeans and a sweater, Libby sat at her desk and pulled out a piece of paper along with the haiku Margaret had given her. Since she had some time to kill, she figured she could work on the poem she wanted to write for Rebecca. She sat there, pen in hand, thinking about what she might possibly say that would make Rebecca understand how much their friendship meant to her.

She scribbled words on the piece of paper only to cross them out a little while later. Over and over again she wrote something and then crossed it out.

Nothing seemed right, and it was even harder than she'd imagined.

When it was fifteen minutes before four o'clock, she stood up and went to the window. Miraculously, the clouds had parted a bit and the rain had stopped. For now, anyway. Libby ran downstairs, grabbed her coat and galoshes, which she hurried to put on, and called out, "Since it's stopped raining, I'm going to take Dexter for a walk."

"Take an umbrella, just to be safe," Aunt Jayne called back.

"All right," she replied. Dexter approached her, so she fastened his lead to his collar. Then she grabbed an umbrella before heading out the front door.

With every step, Libby's stomach felt more anxious. But she knew she couldn't change her mind this time. She had to tell him. It wasn't right to keep this secret from him if she wanted to keep Cedric as a friend. And she did.

She really, really did.

When she got to the park, Cedric was already there, standing next to the play structure. When Libby walked up, she smiled and pointed to the big puddle at the bottom of the slide. "That could be fun, landing in that. Want to try it?"

He stared at the puddle and shook his head. No words came out of his mouth, which seemed strange.

"Cedric?" Libby asked. "Are you all right?"

He didn't say anything for a moment. A long moment. Finally, he looked at her and said, "How come you didn't tell me?"

Libby gulped. "Tell you what?"

"I saw you," he said softly. "Standing in front of the shop, getting your photo taken. With your parents. I mean, your aunt and uncle."

Libby's heart raced as she tried to figure out what to say. Before she could think of anything, Cedric continued, "My mum wanted to see how Mr. Pemberton's is decorated for the holidays. I couldn't believe it when I saw you." He shook his head and looked down at the ground again.

At last Libby found her voice. "I was going to tell you

about it," she said. "Today. I swear. I just didn't know how before. I kept hoping you'd guess my favorite candy, because I thought that would be a perfect time to tell you. But then you couldn't figure it out, and I realized today how wrong it was to keep it from you."

He looked at her again. "How am I supposed to believe you? You've had so many chances to tell me. And you didn't."

"Well, see, I went and saw Margaret again and she said something —"

He held up a hand, interrupting her. "I don't think I can meet you here anymore. Or talk to you at school. I mean, it doesn't seem right. We're on different sides."

Libby had a feeling that wasn't the real reason. He'd trusted her, and Libby knew she'd let him down. Her upset stomach gurgled as she glanced up at the sky. It'd begun to rain again.

She turned her attention back to Cedric. "Please don't talk like that. You make it sound like a comic book story. Like I'm the villain or something."

The rain fell harder. "I gotta go," Cedric said. "I didn't bring an umbrella."

Libby popped hers open. "Here, we can share. It's more than big enough for the two of us."

"It's a little too late to decide you want to share with me now," he said softly. And then he and Goldie turned around and walked away.

Chapter 20

Chocolate Raisin
the taste might surprise you

The last yellow leaf.
Winter is the enemy.
It falls. The tree cries.

The next day, Sunday, Libby stared out her bedroom window, watching as the rain pounded the bare trees. The only haiku she'd written that was halfway decent, in her mind, was one that expressed how sad she felt at what had happened with Cedric. Try as she might, she couldn't write one for Rebecca.

Loneliness filled her. A lot had happened over the past few weeks and all of the missing — for her great-grandma, for Rebecca, and now for Cedric — made her heart hurt.

She got up and reached under her bed to get the box that held all of Grandma Grace's journals. Sometimes her grandma had written about hard times, and Libby thought maybe reading about how she got through them would make her feel better.

She flipped through a couple of the more recent journals, but realized they weren't particularly interesting. The older Grandma Grace had become, the less she'd written.

Libby reached down and pulled one from deep in the stack. The dates on the front told her this one was written about fifteen years ago. It occurred to Libby that this was about the time Grandma Grace had moved out of the house she'd lived in for a really long time. Maybe, Libby thought, she'd written about that experience. It couldn't have been easy, to leave the house she'd loved, filled with so many wonderful family memories.

When Libby cracked open the journal, it opened to a folded piece of paper stuck between the pages, as if it'd been placed there for safekeeping. Libby's heart started racing.

It couldn't be, could it?

Very carefully, Libby unfolded the paper. When she saw

what it was, she let out a loud gasp. Her hands shook as she read the poem she'd previously convinced herself she'd never find.

Friendship is the Sweetest Thing
by Mae Carlisle

A fragrant rose
in a darling vase,
a delicious peach,
a puppy's face.

These things are sweet,
it's oh so true,
but none compare
to a friend like you.

It's rare to have
a friend who cares,
is always there,
who listens and shares.

Wherever you go,
whatever you do,
you're the sweetest of all
and I appreciate you.

"Wow," Libby whispered. She'd found it. She'd actually found it! Grandma Grace must have stuck the poem in the journal and forgotten about it.

Libby read the poem a few more times, wondering what it felt like when Grandma Grace received the special gift from Mae. She must have been so touched by the whole thing.

Libby tried to imagine Rebecca writing her a poem like the one Mae had written, and it almost made her laugh. In all the years she'd known her, Rebecca hadn't done much giving at all. They had played and had fun, like most friends do. But so often, Rebecca was all about . . . Rebecca.

And that's when it hit her. She suddenly knew why she'd had such a hard time writing a poem for Rebecca. If Rebecca had been a good friend, the kind of "friend who cares, is always there, who listens and shares," it would have been much easier to write a sweet poem for her and about her.

The problem was, Rebecca hadn't been that kind of friend. At least, not in a really long time.

With the poem in hand, she returned to her desk and got out a piece of paper. Libby couldn't wait to tell someone about this latest discovery. If anyone would understand how the poem made her feel, she thought it would be Caitlin, since it'd been her small book of poems that Libby and the rest of the girls had fallen in love with at camp.

Dear Caitlin,

Thanks for your recent letter. I'm so glad you are having fun with your new friends — they sound like wonderful girls.

I just read a poem that one of my great-grandma's friends wrote for her a long, long time ago. It's called "Friendship is the Sweetest Thing." I'll have to bring it along to camp next summer and share it during friendship circle. I think my Cabin 7 BFFs will like it a lot.

It might sound strange, but the poem made me think about my friend Rebecca in a new way. I think I've realized it's time to let her go. Have you ever had to do that? Let a friend go?

I feel like maybe I haven't missed my best friend, Rebecca, as much as I've missed simply having a best friend. I mean, I know I have you and Mia and Hannah, but it's hard when you're not here to do things with.

Anyway, now I've upset another friend, and I have to try and figure out how to fix things. I'm hoping the lucky bracelet comes through for me, and everything works out. If only I had a pair of lucky trousers too. (Sorry, you won't know what that means, I know. Long story.)

Oh, I almost forgot — happy holidays!

Write back soon.

Your Cabin 7 BFF,

Libby

Chapter 21

Candy Necklace
a unique fashion accessory

$\mathcal{B}$efore school on Monday, Libby found Sabrina and asked if she'd have lunch with her. She was relieved when Sabrina said yes. After everything that had happened over the weekend, Libby desperately needed to talk to someone.

When they met up, they found a spot at the end of a table where they could sit and chat while eating their lunches from home.

After they sat down, Sabrina said, "I've been dying to know if you found the jar."

Libby smiled. "I did."

Sabrina clapped her hands together. "Oh hooray, the mystery is solved. Did you go to your great-grandma's house and find it there?"

Libby shook her head and then told the story of how she'd come to find the light purple canning jar. Sabrina munched on her sandwich as she listened to the story intently. When Libby finished, Sabrina said, "Wait a second. You couldn't find the jar because it had changed *color*? That is, like, the niftiest thing ever."

Her reaction made Libby laugh. "I know. I might not believe it if I hadn't seen it for myself. And I'm so glad that Margaret let me take the jar home. But you haven't even heard the best part yet. I found the poem Mae had written to Grandma Grace, in one of her old journals. That was the thing I was most interested in, because . . ."

Libby's voice trailed off, as she thought of Rebecca and their friendship troubles. She really didn't want to share those troubles with Sabrina. At least, not right now.

"Because why?" Sabrina asked.

"Because it's more personal," Libby said. "It's a really sweet poem too. In fact, the poem is even titled, 'Friendship is the Sweetest Thing.'"

"Ah," Sabrina said. "I love that. Is it a good poem?"

Libby swallowed a bite of her sandwich and then said, "I think it is. I mean, have you ever tried to write a poem before?

I spent the weekend trying to write haikus, and it's harder than you think. Mae wasn't a professional writer or anything, just a regular girl like you or me, so yeah, it's really good."

"Why were you trying to write haikus?" Sabrina asked.

"Because I was trying to figure out my feelings about some things," Libby said.

"Did it work?" Sabrina asked.

Libby nibbled on an apple slice as she thought about this. "In a way, yes. I wrote one about how sad I am that Cedric is mad at me. That's why I wanted to talk to you today, actually. I could use your help. I have to get him to see how sorry I am."

"Why is he mad at you?" Sabrina asked.

"My family owns Mr. Pemberton's Olde Sweetshop. Cedric's family owns The Sweet Retreat. But when I found that out, I didn't tell him about our sweetshop. I was finally going to, on Saturday, when I met up with him at the park. I'd suddenly realized how wrong it was for me to keep the secret from him. Except he found out about it before I could tell him."

"Uh-oh," Sabrina said as she popped a baby carrot into her mouth. As she chewed, she seemed to be thinking hard. "So tell me about him. What's Cedric like?"

"He's nice. Kind of quiet. He has a dog named Goldie. And, like I told you at the park, he likes to draw. And to read comic books." She thought about his stamp collection, but she knew that wasn't something he'd want Libby to share. "I think he just really likes art. Oh, and he has some lucky trousers." The thought made her happy and sad all at the same time. "I should have told him a long time ago about our sweetshop. I know that now. But I can't go back. All I can do is try to make things right."

"Maybe you should make him a cake or something."

Libby had actually been wracking her brain, trying to think of something Cedric would like. A cake seemed too random, like she could do that for anyone. She wanted to do something special. Unique. Something that showed him she'd really thought about it, and that his friendship meant a lot to her.

When Mae came to visit Grandma Grace all those years ago, she'd probably brought a jar of peaches along because they were one of Grace's favorite things. Grandma Grace had even written in the journal about how much she loved them, and that she could still remember how fun it had been to share the jar of peaches with her friend.

So what could she do that would send the message loud and clear to Cedric that their friendship mattered to Libby? Frustrated, she put her head in her hands and sighed. "If only Lobsterman could come and save the day."

Sabrina chuckled. "Did you say Lobsterman?"

"Yes. He's a character Cedric drew." Just then, Libby sat up straight, as an idea popped into her brain. "Wait a minute. You like to draw. And I like to draw. Although I'm not that good with people or animals. But I could try."

"What are you thinking of doing?"

Libby looked over at the windows that lined one side of the cafeteria. The storm from yesterday had passed. It was cloudy, but dry.

"Do you think you could meet me at the park?" Libby asked. "After school?"

"No problem. Remember, almost every day my mother pushes me outside if it's not raining."

"Could you bring your art supplies too?" Libby asked.

"Sure."

Libby rubbed her hands together. "You know what? I think this is going to be a lot of fun."

Chapter 22

Sour Apple Candy
green like an alien

All week long, Libby and Sabrina met at the park after school, except on Wednesday, when it rained. Libby told her aunt she was meeting a new friend there every day to work on a project and that's why she couldn't take Dexter along. Her aunt said she could invite her friend to come to their house, but Libby and Sabrina liked sitting at the park, talking and laughing and drawing without anyone listening in, even when it was chilly and they had to bundle up.

While they drew, they talked about everything. Their favorite books. Their favorite movies. Their favorite foods. And a hundred other things. The more Libby got to know Sabrina, the more she liked her.

And on top of all that, the project they worked on became more and more amazing each day. They were making a comic book for Cedric called *Goldie and Dexter Save the World.*

It told the story of a spaceship landing in their town of Tunbridge Wells. The townsfolk stayed inside, not sure what to do, hoping the military would take action. But one night, Dexter snuck out of his home and went to get his friend Goldie so she could help him carry out his plan. The two dogs went from neighborhood to neighborhood, gathering up dogs to join their cause. Finally, in the early morning hours, hundreds and hundreds of dogs approached the spaceship. Their barks were deafening. They growled at the aliens any time one of them even peeked his head out of the spacecraft.

The dogs didn't let up. They stayed all day and most of the night, until finally, with the bright crescent moon hanging low in the sky, the spaceship took off and flew back toward space.

The town had a pet parade the next day to celebrate. Dexter and Goldie sat in the front seat of a convertible car, proud little puppies for saving the world. Cedric and Libby sat in the back, where they threw sweets to all the little kids watching the parade. (Libby made sure the candy bag had the words "The Sweet Retreat" on it.) The last lines of the story read, "After the parade, life went back to normal. Cedric and Libby walked their dogs every Saturday afternoon at the park. And whenever they got into a disagreement, it didn't last long, because one thing an alien invasion does is make you appreciate your friends and family a little bit more."

Libby had drawn the funny-looking green aliens and the spaceship. Sabrina had drawn all of the dogs, since she was so good at drawing animals. When they got to the last page, Libby decided she would draw herself and Sabrina would draw Cedric.

"What if he doesn't like how I draw him?" Sabrina asked on Friday as they finished up the comic book.

Libby smiled. "You sound just like Cedric, asking 'what if.' Don't worry, he'll like it."

Sabrina went back to drawing. "I sure hope so. When are you planning on giving it to him anyway?"

"I need to call him and set up a time to meet. If he'll even agree to see me. If not, I guess I'll have to find a way to stuff it into his locker at school or something."

Just then, they heard the words, "Hi, Libby."

Sabrina looked up and Libby turned around, following the voice that had just said hello. It was Rebecca.

"Oh," Libby said. "Hi." She looked around. "Where are all your friends?"

"They're not here yet. Running late, I guess."

"Oh. I see. Uh, Rebecca, this is Sabrina. Sabrina, this is Rebecca."

"Hi!" Sabrina said cheerfully. "Nice to meet you."

Rebecca peered over Libby at the pages on the table. "What are you two doing?"

Before Libby could reply, Sabrina continued on in her cheery voice. "We're making this nifty comic book about an alien invasion and dogs saving the world and . . ."

Her voice trailed off as Libby watched Rebecca's face scrunch up into a look of disgust.

"Why?" Rebecca asked, her face still looking as if someone had just handed her a worm and told her to eat it. "Why would you want to do that?"

Libby stared at Sabrina, trying to come up with a clever response to that question, but she didn't have one. So Sabrina replied with a simple, "Because it's fun?"

Rebecca laughed. "Sure, if you're an eight-year-old boy, maybe."

Libby's blood boiled. Sabrina hadn't done a single thing to deserve to be treated that way. Rebecca had carried on and on about her new friends in conversations with Libby, and not once had Libby said anything unkind. And in less than a minute of meeting a new friend of Libby's, she was going to say something like *that*? Who did she think she was?

"That's not very nice," Libby said as she stood up. "I don't know what's happened to you, Rebecca, but I think you should leave. Go wait for your amazing new friends and leave us alone if you want to act like that."

Rebecca tossed her hair over her shoulder and gave them a ridiculous fake smile. "I was only messing around. Geez. Can't you take a joke?"

Just then, a male voice called out, "Rebecca!" from across the park. She turned to see who it was, then smiled and waved.

"Time for me to go," Rebecca said. "You kids have fun. See ya later."

She rushed off before Libby or Sabrina could say anything else.

"Did she just call us kids?" Sabrina asked.

Libby sighed. "Yep. She sure did. I'm really sorry. It's so embarrassing that she acted that way. Honestly, I don't know what's happened to her."

"How do you know her?"

Libby picked up a green pencil and started coloring in a tree she'd drawn for the last park scene. "We used to be best friends."

Sabrina didn't say anything for a minute. She went to work coloring the bark brown on Libby's tree. "I'm sorry," she said softly. "I know it's hard. Growing apart. Losing a friend."

"Yeah," was all Libby could manage to say. It hurt, thinking of Rebecca as the girl Libby *used to be* friends with. Even if she knew it was for the best.

"Hey," Sabrina said. "I have an idea. Want to see if you can sleep over at my house tonight? I'm sure my mum wouldn't mind. She'd love it, actually. She was just saying earlier today how much she wants to meet you."

Before Libby could answer, the sound of laughter carried across the park as Rebecca and her friends joked about something. A month ago, Libby would have turned around and stared at Rebecca, so envious of all the fun she was having without her. But something had changed. Just like with the purple canning jar, Libby had found something she hadn't quite expected. Or rather, someone.

So today, she didn't turn and stare and feel envious like all of the other times. Today Libby looked at her new friend, smiled, and said, "I'd love to sleep over. Sounds like fun." Then she took a sheet of paper and started writing on it. She counted out syllables on her fingers, thinking hard, wanting to get it right.

Sabrina looked puzzled. "What are you doing?"

"Hold on," Libby said. "I've almost got it."

She wrote more words, erased a couple, then scribbled down some more. Finally, she sat back with satisfaction and passed it to Sabrina.

It said:

A haiku for Sabrina
Friendship is nifty
when you can just be yourself.
I'm glad you're my friend.

Chapter 23

Candy Cane
a Seasonal American favorite

Friday night, after Libby and Sabrina gave each other manicures and pedicures, they sat in Sabrina's room, on the floor, listening to music.

"I think I'm ready to call Cedric," Libby said as she fingered the charm bracelet. She needed it to be lucky now more than ever. "I'd rather call him while you're here with me."

"All right," Sabrina said. She picked her phone up off the floor and handed it to Libby as Libby pulled the piece of paper with Cedric's phone number out of her pocket. She'd grabbed it when she'd gone home to pack for the sleepover.

Libby started to dial and then stopped.

"When I'm scared to do something," Sabrina said, "my mum always asks me, what's the worst thing that can happen? Once we say it out loud, sometimes it doesn't sound as bad as we think it is."

"I'm not sure what that would be," Libby said. "Hang up on me? That would be pretty horrible. Actually, the worst thing that could happen is that he decides to never speak to me again."

"Just get it over with," Sabrina said as she picked up a magazine.

Libby nodded. "Yes. You're right." She dialed quickly and then held the phone to her ear.

It rang once. Twice. Three times. Libby was about to hang up, disappointed and frustrated, when he finally answered.

"Hello?"

"Cedric? It's me, Libby."

"Who?"

"Libby."

"Oh, you mean the girl who kept the biggest secret in the world from me after I told her all kinds of secrets, like how I have a stamp collection and how I still play with action figures and how I believe in lucky trousers? Do you mean that girl? If so, I'm not sure I really have anything to say."

Libby closed her eyes and hung her head. "Cedric, please don't be like that. I'm so very sorry about not telling you about our sweetshop. I still want us to be friends. We can do that, can't we?"

Silence. And then, very quietly, Cedric said, "I don't know. You should have told me. I really wish you'd told me."

"Yes. I was wrong, and I feel so bad. Look, the reason I'm calling is that I have something for you, and I really want to give it to you to show you how sorry I am. Can you meet me at the park tomorrow afternoon?"

"Probably not." Cedric said. "I'm supposed to help out at the shop tomorrow."

Libby wasn't sure if she should believe this or not. Was it just an excuse to make it easy to say no? "Doing what?"

There was a pause. "I can't tell you. You'll laugh."

"I promise I won't laugh."

"You will."

"I won't."

He took a deep breath. "Fine. My mum is completely obsessed with all things American, and so, she's made me a candy cane costume, and I have to wear it to try and bring in customers."

Of all the things Libby thought Cedric might say, this was not one of them. She bit her lip so she wouldn't laugh, trying to picture Cedric dressed up as a candy cane, walking along the sidewalk, trying to lure people into The Sweet Retreat.

"Well, it's very creative," Libby said. "Especially here in England, where we're afraid to do anything that might make us look foolish."

"I guess my mum thinks as long as I'm the one being the fool," Cedric said, "it's fine."

Libby didn't want him to feel worse than he already did about the whole situation. She tried to sound upbeat and positive when she said, "I'm sure you will look very festive, and it will bring in lots of business."

"I hope so," Cedric said softly. "Our shop isn't doing very well. We saw the ad you've been running. I think it's great. I wish we could find something that works for us. I really don't think a silly costume is going to do it, but they're desperate. They'll try anything."

Libby felt a knot in her stomach as she thought of his family, struggling to bring in customers. Why couldn't there be enough business for both of the shops to do well? That's what she wanted. More than anything.

"Have your mum and dad thought about selling other things too? What's that called . . . expanding the business?"

"Not really."

"You know what?" Libby said. "I'm going to come to the shop tomorrow. I want to see it. Maybe you and I can brainstorm ideas on ways you could make the business more successful."

"Libby, you don't have to do that. What if your aunt and uncle find out? They'll be furious with you."

There was that "what if" again. Well, she didn't want to think about that right now. All she wanted was to make things right with Cedric. To help him. Sabrina clapped her hands together, quietly, as if to say, *Way to go*.

"No, it's fine. I want to come and see the place. And see you too. I need to give you this thing I've made you."

"It's not another candy costume, is it?" Cedric said.

Libby smiled. Maybe everything was going to be all right

after all. She hoped so. "No. I promise, it is not another candy costume. Not even close."

"All right. You can stop by. But only if you'll finally tell me your favorite candy." Cedric said.

"Swedish Fish."

"Really?"

"Yep."

"Those are my mum's favorite," he said. "She'll adore you when she hears that."

"We're going to find a way to help your parents," Libby said. "I promise, Cedric. We will."

There had to be a way. There just had to be.

Chapter 24

Cotton Candy
the perfect circus snack

After Libby and Sabrina had muffins and juice for break-fast the next morning, Libby headed for home. The night before, while Sabrina slept in the bunk below, Libby had lain awake, thinking about Cedric, The Sweet Retreat, his parents, and her aunt and uncle.

As hard as it might be to tell the truth, she'd decided she must tell her aunt and uncle about Cedric and the business his parents owned. The last thing she wanted was to have another one of her secrets blow up in her face and cause more people to be angry with her.

At home, Libby greeted Dexter with lots of pats and sweet words. Then she went to the kitchen, where she found her aunt and uncle sitting at the table, sipping on coffee and reading the newspaper.

"Oh good," Libby said. "You haven't left for work yet, Uncle Oliver. I have something I need to tell the both of you."

They both looked at her. "Is everything all right?" Aunt Jayne asked. "Did you have fun at the sleepover?"

Libby sat down. "Yes. This has nothing to do with Sabrina. It's just, I've been thinking about it a lot lately, and I really need to tell you something I've kind of been keeping a secret. And I really hope you aren't too upset after you hear what I have to say."

Uncle Oliver folded the newspaper and set it down. "We're listening."

"I met this boy, Cedric, at the park a while back. He goes to Bennett, too. And Dexter really liked his dog, a cocker spaniel named Goldie. And so Cedric and I started talking and —"

Her aunt and uncle looked at each other in horror and then back at Libby before Aunt Jayne interrupted her. "No. No, no, no. Libby, you are too young to have a boyfriend."

"She's right," Uncle Oliver said. "Far, far too young."

Libby stared at them in disbelief. Then she started laughing. "No, it's not like that at all. I promise. We're just friends."

"Are you certain of that?" he asked. "Because I know boys, and you are a very cute girl, and —"

Libby shook her head. "Please, no. I'm positive. We're friends and nothing more." She paused for a moment, feeling sad about what she was about to say. "I don't know if you've noticed or not, but I've had a bit of a hard time in the friendship department lately." Libby fiddled with her charm bracelet. "Rebecca and I, we aren't close anymore. And Cedric came along at a time when I really needed a friend."

Aunt Jayne rubbed Libby's arm. "I'm sorry, love. I didn't know you and Rebecca had a falling out. I know that must have been hard."

Libby looked up again, hoping she could get them to understand. "It was. But Cedric's really nice. He's easy to talk to. He makes me laugh."

"All right," Uncle Oliver said, taking a drink of coffee. "Well, I suppose having a boy as a friend is all right."

"That makes two new friends then, yes?" Aunt Jayne asked. "Sabrina seems like a very sweet girl."

"Yes," Libby said. "I feel so lucky to have met both of them." She took a deep breath. "But here's what I want to tell you. About Cedric." She paused. "Promise you won't get mad?"

"Just tell us, please," her uncle said.

Libby stuck her finger in the air. "Wait. I think I need a couple of things to help explain all of this. I'll be right back."

She rushed to her room, grabbed Mae's poem along with the haiku she'd written after Cedric had been upset with her, and went back to the table.

"This is quite suspenseful," Aunt Jayne said with a smile. "I hope you aren't going to tell us you've decided to run off to the circus with Cedric."

"Hey, that's a great idea," Libby teased. "He can be a clown, and I can stick my head into the lion's mouth."

"Now anything you tell us will pale in comparison to running away with the circus," Uncle Oliver said. "Job well done, Jayne."

"All right, so, after I met Cedric," Libby explained, "I learned he loves comic books. He loves reading them and he loves making them himself. He's a very good artist. And I learned he has a pair of lucky trousers, and he was willing to loan them to me at one point, that's how nice he is."

Aunt Jayne raised one eyebrow. "They wouldn't have fit you, would they?"

Libby smiled and continued. "Anyway, what I mean by all of that is I learned all of these things about him, and I decided I really liked walking our dogs together. I'd already made up my mind that I wanted to be his friend. Do you see?"

Uncle Oliver scowled. "Yes. But what's the bad news? I can tell it's coming."

Libby talked quickly. "When he told me his parents owned The Sweet Retreat, I didn't tell him about our shop. I kept it a secret from him, because I didn't want it to ruin our friendship. Except he found out about it, and he got very upset with me, and last week he wouldn't speak to me. I wrote this haiku after he found out and got mad, that's how sad I was about the whole thing."

She finally took a breath as she pushed the piece of paper with the haiku out in front of them so they could see it, but they didn't even look at it. They simply stared at Libby looking very, very confused.

"His parents own The Sweet Retreat?" Aunt Jayne asked.

Libby nodded.

Her aunt and uncle looked at each other, as if trying to figure out what to say next. Then Aunt Jayne reached down and picked up the haiku and read it aloud.

"The last yellow leaf.
Winter is the enemy.
It falls. The tree cries."

"In case you can't tell," Libby said, "I was extremely sad when I thought our friendship might be over for good."

"Yes," Aunt Jayne said. "I can tell. It's very well written, Libby, and I could feel the sorrow you felt as you wrote it."

"You see," Libby said, looking at her uncle, who had yet to say anything, "I don't think it should matter that our families are competitors. We're just kids and it's not our fault, right?"

"You said Cedric got upset with you," Uncle Oliver said. "Is he still not speaking to you?"

"That's why I'm telling you all of this," Libby said. "I called him last night, and I want to go to The Sweet Retreat today. I have a comic book that Sabrina and I made for

Cedric, and I want to give that to him, so he knows how sorry I am. But it's more than that. Their business is struggling, and I think Cedric and I should brainstorm ways to help his family. Like, maybe they should sell something else besides just sweets."

"Libby, I know your heart is in the right place," Aunt Jayne said, "but I'm not sure it's wise for you to get involved in their business."

"They might think you have an ulterior motive," Uncle Oliver said.

"I don't know what that means," Libby said.

"It means," her aunt said, "that they might believe you're doing it to benefit our own sweetshop in some way. They might not believe that you're simply doing it out of the kindness of your heart."

Libby narrowed her eyes. "But I am."

"Yes, we know that," Uncle Oliver said. "But they don't. After all, they don't know you at all."

"Well, I'm not planning on telling them anything, just Cedric. And then he can talk to them if he wants to. Anyway, is it all right if I go there this afternoon? After I do my work, refilling the jars?"

Uncle Oliver pointed to the other piece of paper, turned down, on the table. "What's that?"

"Oh, it's another poem. It was written by a friend of Grandma Grace's. It's called 'Friendship is the Sweetest Thing.' And to me, that's true. Friendship is even sweeter than candy." Libby smiled. "And more important too, I think. So can I go? Please?"

Uncle Oliver read Mae's poem and then handed it to Jayne to read.

"Friends are important," Aunt Jayne said when she finished reading. "It's absolutely true."

"That they are," Oliver agreed. "You can go, but only if you let your aunt drive you there. It's across town, and that would be a pretty long bike ride for you."

Libby flung her arms around her uncle's shoulders and said, "Thank you."

When they separated, Uncle Oliver said, "Maybe you should suggest an entirely different business all together. Tell them they should sell luggage or something."

Aunt Jayne wagged her finger at her husband. "Now, now. Let's have none of that."

"I'm sorry, that wasn't very nice of me," Uncle Oliver said. He looked at Libby. "You're a smart girl. I bet you'll come up with a brilliant idea."

Libby rubbed the charm bracelet for luck and said, "I sure hope so."

Chapter 25

Mint Humbug
it's quite different

$\mathcal{L}$ibby's aunt dropped her off across the street from The Sweet Retreat. "I'm going to run some errands, then I'll be back to pick you up," Jayne told her. "I won't be gone long, maybe thirty minutes or so."

"All right. See you soon."

Libby hopped out with her canvas bag that held the comic book and went to the crosswalk. As she waited to cross the street, Cedric came out of the store dressed in his costume. He wore a big, puffy white one-piece suit of some kind, with red diagonal stripes and a tall red-and-white hat that curved at the end, just like a candy cane.

Libby couldn't help but feel sorry for him. He looked pretty ridiculous. He hadn't seemed to notice her walking across the street as he made his way down the sidewalk. Libby stood in front of the candy store entrance, waiting until he turned around and started walking toward her.

She waved and he waved back.

"I think I like your lucky trousers better," she said when he reached her.

"You and me both," Cedric said. "Although with all the stupid things happening lately, I don't think I can call them lucky anymore."

"I'm really sorry," Libby said as she reached into her bag. She pulled out the comic book and handed it to him. "This is for you. I know you probably can't read it right now, because you're working, but maybe later?"

He stared at the front of the comic book, with the funny title and the amazing artwork Sabrina had done.

"You did this?" he asked. "For me?"

"Well, my new friend, Sabrina, helped me. She drew the dogs, since I'm not very good at animals. I drew some of the other things. And I wrote the story."

"Wow," he said softly. "I'm impressed."

Just then, a woman stepped outside. "Cedric, is everything all right? Why'd you stop walking?"

"Oh, Mum, this is my friend Libby. Libby, this is my mother."

"Hi, Libby. I'm Mrs. Arnold," she said. "It's so nice to meet you. Would you like to come in and see our shop?"

"I'd love to," Libby said. She felt relieved Cedric hadn't mentioned Mr. Pemberton's to his mother. It made coming into their shop a lot less awkward.

When they walked in, Libby almost gasped because it was so very different from Mr. Pemberton's. It was bright and modern. Instead of old-fashioned jars, all of the candy was spread out across the shop in tubs with bags so customers could help themselves.

"I've never seen anything like this," Libby said.

"Yes," Mrs. Arnold said, "it's quite different from what we're used to here in England. Shops like this are much more common in America. We wanted to try it, and see if people liked getting the candy themselves rather than having someone else do it for them."

Libby walked around, looking at the different types of candy they had. When she found her favorite, she took a scoop and counted out ten of the colorful fish and put them in a bag. She'd brought along some of her allowance, because she didn't want to be rude and not buy anything.

"Ah, a girl after my own heart," Mrs. Arnold said when Libby took her bag of candy to the register. "Is there anything else you'd like?"

"This is all for now, thank you," Libby replied as she reached for her wallet.

"Oh no, it's my treat," Mrs. Arnold said. "I'm glad you came to visit us and see our shop."

Libby stuck the candy in her bag. "That's really nice of you. Thanks."

"My pleasure."

Behind where Mrs. Arnold stood, a cute plaque hung on the wall that said, I'LL TAKE THREE SCOOPS OF KINDNESS, PLEASE. Beneath those words was a small ice cream cone with three hearts stacked on top of each other, like three scoops of ice cream.

"I like that plaque behind you," Libby said.

"Thank you," Mrs. Arnold replied. "A friend of mine gave it to me for my birthday. I figured we could hang it here, even if we're scooping candy and not ice cream."

Libby looked over at Cedric, but he was busy reading his

comic book. Should she mention the idea that had just popped into her head, or wait and tell Cedric later, when they were alone? Something told her she should tell her, right now. After all, what did she have to lose?

"With a name like The Sweet Retreat, it seems like you could sell ice cream pretty easily too. Kids are crazy for ice cream, you know. Maybe even more so than candy."

Mrs. Arnold stuck her hands into the pockets of the bright yellow apron she wore around her waist. "Ice cream?" she asked, as if she was trying this idea on for size.

"Yes. Just think. On one side of your shop, you could have candy. And on the other side, ice cream by the scoop."

Cedric came over and stood next to Libby. "Mum, I think that is a brilliant idea. We've been trying to think of how we can make more money. If we sold ice cream too, you wouldn't have to change the name or anything."

"We'd have to rearrange some things and add some freezer cases," Mrs. Arnold said as she looked around the room, like she was trying to imagine what it would look like. "Your father's in the back, doing some paperwork. I'll have to talk to him about this idea a little bit later." She smiled. "I like it. I really do. Thank you, Libby, for mention-ing it."

"You're welcome," Libby said. She looked at Cedric and then back at Mrs. Arnold, as a funny feeling nagged at her. She knew that feeling. It was the same one she'd ignored when Cedric had first told Libby about The Sweet Retreat. After everything she'd been through with Cedric, she didn't want to mess things up again. Even though it would be hard, she knew she should tell Cedric's mum the truth.

"Mrs. Arnold," Libby said. "There's something I need to tell you. My aunt and uncle, who I live with, own the other sweetshop in town. Mr. Pemberton's?" A look of surprise washed over Mrs. Arnold's face, but Libby kept talking. "I still want to be friends with Cedric because we get along so well, and it's not our fault our families are competitors. I'm hoping that might be all right with you?"

Mrs. Arnold looked at her son. He smiled at her, and Mrs. Arnold's face relaxed. She looked back at Libby. "Of course it's all right. I don't want you to feel bad about any-thing. After all, Cedric's father and I are the ones who decided to open this business despite the competition. We simply hoped there would be enough customers to go around."

"I hope there are," Libby said.

"I'm curious, though," Mrs. Arnold said, "about the suggestion you made. Have your aunt and uncle ever considered selling ice cream at Mr. Pemberton's?"

"Oh, no. We would never sell anything but candy in our shop. My uncle is all about keeping up the family tradition. Besides, we don't have nearly as much room as you do. I want your business to do well." Libby's eyes begged Cedric's mother to believe her. "I really do."

"I appreciate that," she replied. "Like I said, I think you've brought up a good idea, and we'll definitely consider it."

"Come on," Cedric said as he walked around behind the counter and slipped the comic book into a drawer. "Let's go back outside so I can make a fool of myself some more."

"I'm happy to help you with that," Libby said. "Goodbye, Mrs. Arnold. Thanks again for the Swedish Fish."

"Good-bye, Libby."

When they got outside, Cedric said, "Well, that was something."

Libby smiled. It felt like she'd just set down a ton of bricks she'd been carrying around. She felt so much better, now that everything was out in the open. "Your mum is really nice. And I love your shop."

"Thanks," Cedric said. "For everything. The comic book is really great. I love it."

"You're welcome," Libby replied. "So, am I forgiven?"

"Yes. I mean, you didn't even make fun of me when you saw me in this silly costume. That's what I call a good friend."

Libby breathed a sigh of relief. Everything was going to be fine. Well, hopefully everything.

"Do you think they'll do it?" Libby asked. "Do you think your parents will decide to sell ice cream too?"

"I don't know. It's hard to say. But whatever happens, it's a fantastic idea. And you've got them thinking, which is good."

"It might be hard to believe, coming from someone who works at the other sweetshop in town, but I meant what I said about wanting The Sweet Retreat to do well."

"I could probably have mum make you a candy cane costume," Cedric said with a smile. "Or, how about a Swedish

Fish costume? You've always wanted to dress up as a fish, haven't you?"

Libby laughed. "You're on your own there, Cedric. Sorry."

He waved at a passing car. "Thanks, Lib. Thanks a lot." He turned and smiled at her. "Some friend you are."

Chapter 26

Chocolate Coin
rich in taste only

On Sunday, Libby sat at the desk in her room and pulled out a piece of paper. Then she took off the bracelet and set it right in front of her, so she could look at it as she wrote the letter to Hannah. She knew it was time to send it on, especially if she wanted Hannah to receive it before Christmas, which she did. But she was still a little sad about it. The bracelet had become like a part of her. She'd worn it every day and every night, never taking it off, except for the one time she'd put it on the other wrist so she could have a special memory.

She fingered the shiny new charm she'd added to the bracelet yesterday. When her aunt had picked her up from The Sweet Retreat, Libby has asked her if they could go

175

shopping at the nearby jewelry store. It hadn't taken Libby long at all to decide what charm she wanted to add to the bracelet, to join the flower and the bird. It looked so cute and felt absolutely right, after everything that had happened the past month or so.

Dear Hannah,

Hooray, it's your turn to wear the bracelet! Are you excited? I'm excited for you. You've been so patient, waiting for it to be your turn, I hope having three adorable charms to wear on the bracelet makes the wait worth it.

You can probably guess who chose which charm, but just in case, I'll tell you. Caitlin chose the flower charm, Mia chose the bird, and I chose the peppermint candy.

So why the piece of candy? Because, like an old poem I recently found says, "Friendship is the sweetest thing." I feel so lucky to call you and Mia and Caitlin friends. I also feel lucky because I have two new friends, Sabrina and Cedric. I'm going to try and get them to go Christmas caroling with me sometime soon. We'll see what they say. Maybe I'll ask Cedric to wear the candy cane costume his mother made for him to help promote their business. I'm sure he'd love that.

Along with the bracelet, I'm also sending you a bag of dew drops from Mr. Pemberton's Olde Sweetshop. I think in America, you call them gum drops. As you can see, I picked out a variety of flavors for you. Anyway, I hope you like them. You can share them with your family if you want to, but it's perfectly fine if you keep them all for yourself. Just don't eat them all at once. I've learned the hard way that's never a good idea, no matter how good the candy tastes.

That's so wonderful you might get a horse for Christmas. You have to write to me as soon as you find out and tell me if your wish comes true.

Merry Christmas! I miss you!!

Your Cabin 7 BFF,

Libby

As she carefully wrapped the bracelet in some tissue paper, Libby looked over at the purple jar that sat on the nearby nightstand. Sometimes she wondered how much the jar was worth, but of course, it didn't really matter because she'd never consider selling it. To her, the happy feelings she got just by looking at it were worth far more than any amount of money she might get for it.

Once again, thinking about the jar made her think of her great-grandma and her good friend, Mae. One had lived in America while the other one had lived in England, and yet, across all of those miles, they'd managed to stay friends through the years. That's what she wanted with her Camp Brookridge friends, more than anything.

Someday, years and years from now, would a young girl study the charm bracelet and wonder why it had meant so much to a great-grandma and her friends?

Libby smiled as she thought to herself, *That would be awfully sweet.*

Turn the page for a sneak peek
at Hannah's *Charmed Life*!

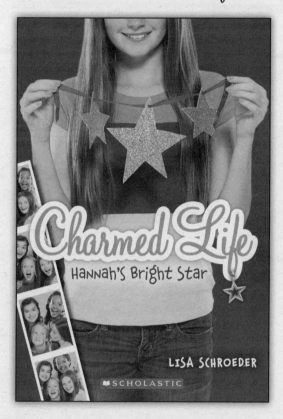

Chapter 1

CONSTELLATION: Andromeda
daughter of Cassiopeia

"Y'all are kidding, right?" Hannah asked as she searched under the Christmas tree for one last box. A box that would have a note in it, telling her to head out to the barn, where she would find the horse she'd always dreamed of. The horse she was absolutely, positively getting for Christmas this year.

She'd overheard her parents talking one night, as she walked by their bedroom. All right, fine, maybe she hadn't heard them mention the word "horse," but she'd heard her mama say, "It's a pretty big responsibility. Are you sure Hannah is ready for it?"

Her daddy had assured her mama that Hannah was, indeed, ready for it, and that was all Hannah had needed to hear. After all, what other big responsibility could they have been talking about it?

Her ears had been pierced since third grade.

She already owned a cell phone.

She wasn't old enough to drive.

It had to be a horse, Hannah had reasoned every single day from that night until now. It just had to be.

She crawled around the Christmas tree, pushing the mess of red, white, and green wrapping paper out of the way as she went, searching for the last box.

"Hannah," her father, Mr. Crawford, said gently from his place on the sofa, next to her mother. "There isn't another box to open. I'm sorry if you're disappointed."

With a heavy sigh, Hannah stopped looking and plopped down on the floor. She yanked on her flannel pajama top covered in penguins, straightening it out. "I am not disappointed. I'm . . . impatient. I love the gifts I've opened so far and I appreciate them, I really do, but I have a feeling there's one more. Isn't there?"

All of the gifts under the tree had been opened. The family had taken turns, to make the best part of Christmas morning last as long as possible. Her older brothers, twins

Adam and Eric, were oblivious to Hannah's desperate pleas, as they had spent the last ten minutes trying to open the box that held the new video gaming system they'd received.

Hannah glanced over at her small pile of gifts, which included an adorable pair of red cowboy boots, a cookie cookbook, an apron, and a necklace with an emerald pendant (her birthstone).

"Please," she begged. Hoping for some luck, Hannah fingered the charm bracelet hanging on her wrist that she'd received from her camp friend Libby last week. "What do I have to do to get you to give it to me? I know there's one more. I just know it."

Grandpa chuckled from his place on the loveseat, next to Grandma. They lived on the same property as Hannah and her family, in the original old farmhouse, right next door. Because of their close proximity, she saw them every day, and she was thankful for that. They were two of her most favorite people in the world.

Now, Hannah eyed the two of them suspiciously. Neither of her grandparents had said a single word the past few minutes. And that wasn't like them. At all.

She made her way over to the loveseat and, while on her

hands and knees, clasped her hands together out in front of her. "Grandpa, do you like seeing me crawl around here like a beggar? What do I have to do? Tell me. Please?"

He smiled as he pointed at the tree. "Say, what is that, stuck between a couple of branches? I can't quite tell from here."

Hannah shrieked as she stood up and dashed over to the tree, stumbling over Grandpa's box of new slippers. "Where?" she cried, her hands batting at the tree branches, the scent of pine circling around her.

"Careful," her mother, Mrs. Crawford, said. "Some of those ornaments have been in my family a long time. I'd be sad to see one of them fall to the floor and break."

Something white caught Hannah's eye, tucked on a branch near the trunk, way up high. "I don't know if I can reach it," she said as she stood on her tippy-toes, stretching herself inward and upward, needles poking her cheek as she did.

And then, she had it. She grabbed whatever it was and pulled it toward her until she could see exactly what it was: an envelope.

She jumped up and down, hugging the envelope to her chest. "I knew it, I knew it!"

"What is it?" Adam asked as he brushed his long, blond bangs out of his gray-blue eyes.

"It better not be money," Eric said. "Unless there are two more envelopes just like that one stuck in there somewhere."

Adam looked at Eric. "Maybe we should look."

"It's not money," Hannah said as she tore open the envelope.

"How do you know?" Adam asked.

"I'm curious about that as well," her father mumbled.

"I just have a feeling, okay?" Hannah pulled out a purple piece of paper. "Aw, my favorite color." She unfolded the paper and read the words out loud.

"There's one last gift
that's not under the tree,
so head out to the barn
where you'll squeal with glee."

Hannah dropped the purple note, grabbed her new cowboy boots, and slipped them on over her pajama bottoms. "Who's going out with me?"

"I reckon I'll go," Grandpa said as he stood up. He reached for Grandma's hand. "And I know your grandma doesn't want to miss this either."

"We'll go too," Mr. Crawford said as both he and Mrs. Crawford stood up.

Hannah clapped her hands. "You folks are slower than maple syrup, you know that? Come on, hurry up." She looked at her brothers. "Don't you want to see what it is?"

"Not right now," Eric said.

"Yeah, maybe later," Adam said. "Mama, I'm hungry. Can we have one of Grandma's cinnamon rolls now?"

"I suppose," Mrs. Crawford replied.

"Just save some for the rest of us," Grandpa said.

"Who can eat at a time like this?" Hannah cried, grabbing her gray wool coat from the hall closet. "Let's go!"

She'd dreamed of this moment forever, it seemed.

And her dream was finally, *finally* coming true.